# The Mona Lisa Mystery

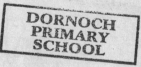

P6

# The Mona Lisa Mystery

## PAT HUTCHINS

### illustrated by

## LAURENCE HUTCHINS

Young Lions
*An Imprint of HarperCollins Publishers*

*Other books by*
*Pat and Laurence Hutchins*
*in Young Lions*

Follow That Bus!
The Curse of the Egyptian Mummy

First published in the USA by Greenwillow Books,
a division of William Morrow and Company, Inc., 1981
First published in Great Britain by The Bodley Head Ltd 1981
First published in Young Lions 1987
Seventh impression September 1992

Young Lions is an imprint of the Children's Division,
part of HarperCollins Publishers Ltd,
77–85 Fulham Palace Road, Hammersmith,
London W6 8JB

Printed and bound in Great Britain by
HarperCollins Manufacturing, Glasgow

For Miss Klaar,
Mr. Lytton
and the children
of New End School

# CONTENTS

# 1

# Paris, Here We Come

The G.B. plates sparkled in the early morning sun as Class 3 of Hampstead Primary School gathered beside the school bus parked in New End Square. Mr. Coatsworth, the driver, had fixed a sign that said "Paris, here we come!" onto the front window of the bus, and was standing back to admire it.

Mr. Jones, the class teacher, was busy collecting passports from the children, who were jostling one another impatiently and talking excitedly about their school trip as they waited to board the bus.

Avril, who had been studying the church clock, pushed herself to the front of the class.

"Where's Miss Parker?" she demanded. "She said if we weren't here by eight o'clock the bus would leave without us. Well, it's eight o'clock now and she ain't here," she added, glancing anxiously up the hill at an approaching taxi in case

Miss Parker was in it. To her relief, nobody got out as the taxi pulled into the kerb.

"Yes sir," chorused the rest of Class 3, pushing eagerly towards the bus door. "Let's go without her!"

Mr. Jones held his hand up for silence. "Miss Parker isn't coming on the bus. But—" he raised his voice above the cheers—"she's meeting us at the ferry. She said," he continued, as the children groaned, "that she'd make her own way to Dover."

Jessica sighed. "And I thought she'd been kidnapped, like that film on Saturday."

"Kidnapped!" Morgan repeated bitterly. "Who'd want to kidnap *her*? They'd have to be mad!"

"And speak French," muttered Sacha, noticing a sleek French car pulling into the square. "She doesn't seem to understand much English."

"Perhaps we could find a mad Frenchman who'd do it," said Matthew thoughtfully, turning to Sacha. "Your dad's half French, isn't he?"

"Yes," said Sacha, "but he isn't mad. Not even half mad," he added quickly.

"Now, children," said Mr. Jones sternly, "I know it's a great shame that Miss Barker can't be with us, but I'm sure that once we've got to know her better, Miss Parker will turn out to be very . . ." His voice trailed off, as the children shuffled their feet. "Quite," he corrected himself, "pleasant. After all, she's only been with us for a few days, and Miss Barker did recommend her. Her French is perfect," he added desperately.

"Her English ain't," said Avril.

Mr. Coatsworth, who had been walking round the bus, polishing the G.B. plates, had heard only part of the conversation. "What's Miss Barker done to you then?" he asked. "I thought she was one of your favourites."

"We're not talking about Miss Barker," said Avril. "We're talking about Miss *Parker*!"

"Barker, Parker," said Mr. Coatsworth, confused. "Who's Miss Parker then? I thought your headmistress was coming. She always comes to France."

"She was," Mr. Jones sighed. "But she was taken to hospital on Thursday with suspected appendicitis. Apparently she rang Miss Parker to ask if she would substitute for her until she was back at school."

"Oh! What a shame!" said Mr. Coatsworth. "We'll have to send her lots of postcards."

"We can't," said Mr. Jones. "We don't know which hospital she's in. She forgot to tell Miss Parker."

"And now horrible Miss Parker is taking us for French until Miss Barker comes back," said Matthew.

"And she's coming with us instead," Sacha

muttered. "Worse luck!"

"Well now," said Mr. Coatsworth cheerfully. "Surely she wouldn't want to come with us if she was that bad!"

"She's probably coming to make sure we're all miserable," said Jessica. "She's probably planning to lock us in the Bastille and watch us slowly starve to death."

"Like the first day she was at school," said Morgan.

"We hadn't done nothing, neither," said Avril indignantly. "We only asked if she came from Paris!"

"She eats an awful lot of garlic," Akbar explained.

"And she don't speak proper, neither," Avril insisted. "She started shouting about being born in Potters Bar, and never having been to Paris in her life, and what name was more English than Parker, then made us stay in and miss lunch."

"Perhaps the poor woman was feeling a bit nervous," Mr. Coatsworth said. He laughed. "I'd be a bit nervous myself meeting you lot for the first time!"

"Anyway," said Mr. Jones, patting Avril's

shoulder, "I'm sure we'll have a marvellous time in Paris. Now, everyone on the bus. We don't want to miss the ferry."

And after they'd all climbed onto the bus, Class 3 forgot all about the new French teacher.

"Paris, here we come!" they screamed, as the bus pulled out of the square.

"Sacha," said Morgan, glancing out of the back window, and prodding Sacha, who was sitting next to him, "didn't your dad say 75 was a Paris registration number?"

"Yes," said Sacha.

"What a coincidence," Morgan murmured.

Sacha looked at the taxi that was driving behind them.

"The black Citroën," said Morgan, "behind the taxi. It has a Paris number plate!"

# 2
# Followed

By the time the bus had reached Dover, the children were beside themselves with excitement.

Jessica didn't stop talking throughout the journey. She told amazing stories about her adventures in the city, and as she was the only child in the class who'd been there (apart from Sacha, who, Jessica pointed out, didn't count, as he was eighteen months old at the time), everyone listened.

"Fancy that!" Mr. Coatsworth would murmur from the driver's seat, as Jessica, ignoring the interruptions from some of the disbelieving children, launched into another hair-raising tale about Paris.

Morgan, who was beginning to have doubts about Jessica's Hunchback of Notre Dame episode himself, glanced idly out of the window.

"Sacha!" he hissed. "Look!" He pointed to the road behind them.

"What? The taxi?" Sacha asked in surprise.

"Behind the taxi," said Morgan.

Cruising behind the taxi was the black Citroën they'd seen earlier, and bending over the wheel was a man with a huge beard.

"I'm sure he's following us," Morgan whispered. "I wonder why."

"Not long now, kids," Mr. Coatsworth shouted, interrupting Morgan's thoughts and Jessica's story, as he pointed to the sign for the ferry.

"He's not following us now," said Sacha. The bus had turned into the traffic lane for the ferry and was immediately overtaken by the taxi, and then by the French car.

"Come on!" he added, as the rest of the children raced to the front of the bus to try and get a glimpse of the ferry. Morgan stood up slowly, shook his head, then ran to the front of the bus too.

The bus stopped at Passport Control while the Immigration officer checked the passports, then wishing them a pleasant journey, told Mr.

Coatsworth to join the line of lorries and buses in front of them.

"There it is!" screamed the children, pointing ahead to the ferry. "And it's boarding!"

"Well done, old girl," said Mr. Coatsworth, patting the steering wheel. "Perfect timing!"

"Perfect," agreed Mr. Jones as the bus followed the line of vehicles down the ramp and onto the ferry.

"And now," he said, when the bus was safely on the boat, "to find Miss Parker." Class 3, groaning at the mention of Miss Parker, followed Mr. Jones and Mr. Coatsworth along the rows of parked vehicles towards the stairs that led to the decks. Suddenly Morgan stopped.

"Sacha!" he cried, pulling his friend back and pointing to a gap between two lorries.

"Crikey!" whispered Sacha.

Parked in the next row was the black Citroën with Paris number plates.

"Come on, lads!" Mr. Jones shouted. "We don't want to lose you already!"

"We're being followed!" Sacha shouted back, but as the rest of Class 3 were crowding round the teacher, all talking at once, he didn't hear Sacha,

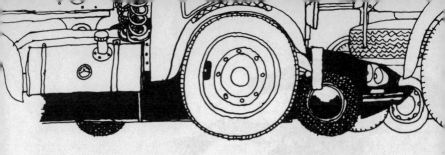

and by the time the two boys had caught up with him, they were already upstairs.

"Mr. Jones," Morgan said breathlessly, "we're being followed!"

"By a bearded man in a black Citroën," said Sacha.

"With Paris number plates," Morgan added.

"I saw a taxi following us," Avril complained, "but I didn't see no Citroën."

"I saw it," shouted Matthew, "in New End Square."

"I saw it too!" cried Akbar.

"So did we!" shouted the rest of Class 3.

Mr. Coatsworth scratched his head. "Come to think of it," he murmured, "I seem to remember seeing a black Citroën in New End. It followed the old girl on the motorway for a while, then overtook her."

"It must just be a coincidence," Mr. Jones said, frowning. "Why would anyone want to follow us?"

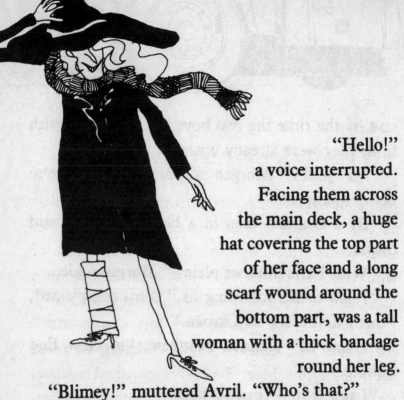

"Hello!"
a voice interrupted.
Facing them across
the main deck, a huge
hat covering the top part
of her face and a long
scarf wound around the
bottom part, was a tall
woman with a thick bandage
round her leg.

"Blimey!" muttered Avril. "Who's that?"

A sudden gust of wind tore the hat from the woman's head. Mr. Jones and the children gasped in amazement. It was Miss Parker who was smiling at them, and her hair, which they had glimpsed before she'd had time to grab her hat and jam it on again, was a brilliant shade of yellow.

"Blimey!" Avril gasped. "She's gone and dyed her hair!"

# 3
# The Bearded Stranger

Mr. Jones and the children stepped back nervously as Miss Parker glided towards them, but Mr. Coatsworth stood transfixed. The same gust of wind that had blown the hat off blew the fragrance of expensive French perfume into his nostrils.

"I don't think you've met Mr. Coatsworth," Mr. Jones said quickly, as the children, who had been studying Miss Parker in shocked silence, recovered and started whispering to one another, and glancing in disbelief at the silky smile on the French teacher's face.

"H-how do you do?" stammered Mr. Coatsworth, holding out his hand. Miss Parker, holding onto her hat with one hand, placed the other limply in his.

"*Bonjour!*" she murmured huskily. "I'm Miss Parker." Then looking down at her hand, she pulled it quickly away, hesitated, then grasped Mr. Coatsworth's hand in a firm handshake. "A jolly good evening. What ho!" she exclaimed heartily.

"It ain't evening, Miss," said Avril, scowling at Mr. Coatsworth, who was still gazing at Miss Parker. "It's morning!"

Miss Parker's eyes narrowed as she looked at Avril, and Avril, who was beginning to wish she hadn't been so bold, took a step backward. The expression on Miss Parker's face changed as Mr. Coatsworth seemed to come out of his trance.

"Oh golly!" she sighed. "Of course it is the morning still. What a silly little girl I am. And what a clever little girl you are," she added, flashing a brilliant smile at Avril, who only edged farther away.

"I am so tired. When one is so tired, one forgets what time of day it is. I had such a little sleep last night," she continued, glancing down at her bandaged leg. "I'm afraid silly me spilled boiling fat all over my poor leg. Cooking chips and fish. I adore chips and fish."

"Perhaps you shouldn't have come," said Mr. Jones anxiously, as the children, unmoved, eyed Miss Parker suspiciously.

"What? And miss this wonderful trip," Miss Parker cried gaily, "with all these wonderful children? Never!"

"How about a nice cup of tea?" Mr. Jones, surprised at having his class described as wonderful, couldn't think of anything else to say. "We can watch the ferry leave from the refreshment room."

Morgan, still puzzling over the bearded man, suddenly whistled. "Look!" he shouted, pointing to a doorway.

Class 3 gazed open-mouthed. From the other side of the boat a bearded face was peering in their direction through a pair of binoculars.

"It's that man again!" Morgan cried.

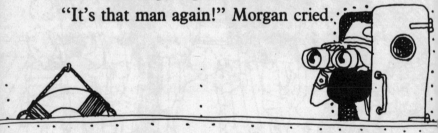

The children blinked as the sun's reflection on the lenses dazzled them, but when they opened their eyes again, ready to give chase, the man had disappeared.

Miss Parker, who had only glimpsed the face, sank heavily onto a bench.

"I think poor Miss Parker must be feeling seasick," said Mr. Coatsworth, as the ferry bumped gently, then glided smoothly away from the dock.

"I'll go and get her a nice hot drink."

"Pardon," said a deep voice behind them.

An enormous swarthy man, who had been standing close to them cleaning his fingernails with a knife, stepped forward. His gold teeth glinted as he smiled at them. Then, producing a French-English phrase book from his pocket, he flicked through it with his knife and slowly said, "I-need-a-doc-tor." He ran his thick finger down the page. "Pardon," he repeated. "I-am-a-doc-tor," he corrected himself, and bent over Miss Parker. None of them noticed a second bearded man picking his way through the crowds behind them.

# 4
# The Search

Miss Parker declined the coffee that Mr. Coatsworth had brought for her, but gulped the brandy from the hip flask that the French doctor offered her.

The children were all for spreading out to look for the bearded stranger, but Mr. Jones said that as the doctor had insisted on staying with Miss Parker until she felt better and as it was twelve o'clock, he'd rather they all stayed together and went to the refreshment room to have their packed lunches.

They left the doctor and Miss Parker talking quietly together in French. "Well!" said Mr. Jones, when the children were eventually seated in the refreshment room, so busy talking about the bearded stranger and the peculiar appearance and behaviour of Miss Parker that their cups of tea were getting cold. "I think the bearded man was only looking for porpoises."

"Why was he hanging around Hampstead then?" Avril demanded. "There ain't no porpoises in Hampstead."

"Oh!" cried Jessica. "Perhaps he's planning to kidnap us and hold us for ransom for a million dollars."

"Who'd want to pay a million dollars for us?" said Matthew.

"Miss Parker!" shrieked Jessica, jumping up again and knocking over the bottle of tomato ketchup that Avril had insisted on bringing with her.

"Would she?" asked Akbar in surprise.

"No!" said Jessica scornfully. "The bearded stranger wants to kidnap *her*! You said—" Jessica stabbed her finger at Morgan—"that only a mad Frenchman would want to kidnap her. Well," she continued breathlessly, "he looked mad to me! And," she added, stabbing her finger at Morgan again, "*you* said he was driving a French car."

"Yes," said Morgan thoughtfully, "but if it was Miss Parker he was after, what was he doing in Hampstead?"

Mr. Jones and Mr. Coatsworth opened their mouths to speak, but Jessica, squealing with excitement, jumped up again. "That's why she's dyed her hair!" she screamed. "So the kidnapper wouldn't recognize her. She's pretending to be a different person!"

"And acting nice when she ain't," Avril muttered.

"And wearing that big hat and scarf," Akbar added, "so the kidnapper couldn't see her face."

"And coming to Paris with us," murmured Matthew, "so he won't find her."

"And *he*'s wearing a false beard so *she* wouldn't recognize him!" Sacha shouted. "That's it, Morgan!"

But Morgan only shook his head slowly. "I don't think so," he said softly.

"Neither do I," said Mr. Jones. "I think the bearded man just happened to be leaving Hampstead the same time as us to catch the ferry. He probably comes from Paris, which explains the Paris number plates. He just happened to be looking through his binoculars when we saw him. And Miss Parker has dyed her hair because she prefers yellow hair to black. And I also think," he finished, "that you should eat your sandwiches before they go stale."

Class 3 (apart from Morgan, who was sitting

with a puzzled frown on his face) were still convinced that there was a kidnapper on board the boat, and were too excited to eat very much.

When it was obvious that the children didn't want to finish their lunch, Mr. Jones said they could go and look round the boat while he and Mr. Coatsworth went to see how Miss Parker was, but they were to meet on the main deck when the ferry arrived at Calais.

Some of the children had heard there was a fruit machine in the bar, and decided that was as good as any place to keep an eye open for the bearded stranger, and perhaps to win a bit of extra pocket money at the same time.

Akbar, Avril and Jessica decided to look in the restaurant, in case he was lurking in there, and Morgan, Matthew and Sacha thought they'd try the top deck and work their way down.

"What are we going to do if we see him?" Sacha asked, as they climbed up the stairs. "We can't just go up to him and ask him if he's a kidnapper." He paused. "And he's not likely to say yes, even if he is."

"I'm not sure he is a kidnapper," said Morgan, as he made his way with Sacha and Matthew

through the crowds of people who had gone up to the top deck to see the shores of France, which were now in view.

"Then what do you think he's up to?" Matthew asked.

Morgan shook his head. "I don't know," he admitted.

They circled the top deck, carefully studying everyone that came up the steps, but they could see no sign of the stranger.

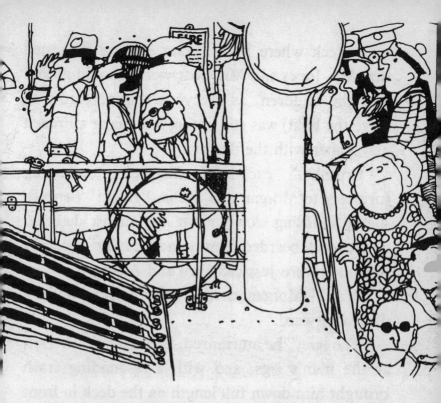

"I suppose we'd better go back to the main deck," said Matthew, as the ferry approached Calais Docks. "We'll be landing soon."

"Well, he's certainly not up here," said Morgan, taking a final look at the passengers. "I'd recognize that beard anywhere."

"Maybe one of the others has spotted him," said Sacha as they made their way down the steps.

"They're not there yet," said Matthew, leaning over the side of the steps and looking down at the

31

main deck where Miss Parker (having suggested that Mr. Jones and Mr. Coatsworth should go and find the children, as everyone was preparing to leave the boat) was still sitting looking at a French newspaper with the doctor.

"Crumbs!" exclaimed Matthew, beckoning furiously to Morgan and Sacha. "Look!" Beneath them, shuffling slowly along the almost deserted deck, was a bearded figure, and creeping stealthily behind it were Jessica, Avril and Akbar.

"Wait!" Morgan cried, as Sacha and Matthew darted forward.

"Too late," he murmured, as Avril threw herself at the man's legs, and with a resounding crash brought him down full length on the deck in front of the doctor and Miss Parker.

# 5
# Mistaken Identity

Miss Parker and the doctor glanced at each other in alarm as Jessica and Akbar, joined by Matthew and Sacha, started tugging furiously at the man's beard.

Morgan, who had been watching in dismay, ran down the steps calling to them, but the man's shrieks drowned his words.

"What on earth is going on?" shouted Mr. Jones, who was running towards them, followed by Mr. Coatsworth and the rest of Class 3, all yelling and adding to the uproar.

"We've caught the kidnapper!" Jessica shouted, yanking at the beard again. Morgan, who still couldn't be heard as everyone was shouting at once, put his fingers to his lips and blew. Everyone fell silent at the piercing whistle. "Jessica," he said, "you've got the wrong man. That's not the man who was following us."

The man sat up as the children loosened their grip on him. His eyes narrowed as he glared at Miss Parker and the doctor.

"Did you put these kids up to this?" he demanded.

"No!" snapped Miss Parker, glancing at the door again. "It was a most terrible mistake. Everything," she added quickly.

"It had better be," he muttered, rubbing his chin as Mr. Jones and Mr. Coatsworth, apologizing profusely, helped him up.

"I'm terribly sorry," said Mr. Jones, as the man straightened his tie, his eyes darting nervously from the children to Miss Parker and then to the doctor. "I can't think what came over the children."

"We thought we was helping," said Avril stoutly. "We thought he was a kidnapper."

"That's why we tried to pull his beard off," said Akbar meekly. "We thought it was a false one."

"So Miss Parker wouldn't recognize him," Jessica added.

"What's all this nonsense and stuff about kidnappers?" Miss Parker demanded. "Why should I not recognize him?" She turned to the bearded man. "I told you it was all a terrible mistake!" she hissed.

The doctor, who had been silent throughout the commotion, was opening his phrase book again. "I-am-a-doc-tor," he said. The bearded man snorted as the doctor's eyes travelled down the book.

"I-will-take-you-for-a-glass-of-bran-dy."

"And I will come also," said Miss Parker softly, "and explain to you everything." She glanced at Mr. Jones. "This poor man is shocked. I will try to calm him down."

The bearded man scowled. "You won't calm me down very easily," he muttered. "But there's a lot of explaining you can do."

The children, having been made to apologize,

35

gazed after them forlornly as Miss Parker and the doctor led the complaining man to the bar.

"Let that," said Mr. Jones sternly, "be a lesson to you. I don't want to hear any more about bearded strangers, kidnappers or disguises. Nothing! Nothing!" he repeated, raising his voice above Jessica's who kept interrupting.

"But, sir!" cried Jessica again, shaking his arm. "Look!"

Creeping towards the bar was another bearded man.

"Crikey!" exclaimed Morgan. "*That's* the one who was following us!"

"After him!" screamed Avril, but the man, having heard Avril's cry, turned, and seeing the crowd of children preparing to follow him, slipped into a doorway and disappeared.

"Oh no you don't!" Mr. Jones thundered.

"But he's getting away," protested Avril.

"If I had a beard," said Mr. Jones grimly, "I'd want to get away from you lot too. The poor fellow obviously saw what you did to the other unfortunate chap. Now, I want no more of this nonsense, no more attacks on innocent passengers, and no more arguments," he added, as Jessica opened her mouth to speak, but, thinking better of it, closed it again.

Class 3 huddled together, gloomily watching the crew preparing the ferry for landing.

Mr. Jones and Mr. Coatsworth talked quietly together, frowning occasionally as they glanced towards the children.

"It's funny," Morgan murmured. "A second bearded stranger turning up, and the first one disappearing."

A loudspeaker announcement, informing all passengers to return to their vehicles, interrupted him.

Mr. Jones and Mr. Coatsworth joined the group of children.

"When Miss Parker gets back," said Mr. Jones, "we'll get you lot onto the bus where I can keep my eye on you." He paused, looking around for the French teacher, but couldn't see her among the people making their way to the vehicles.

"Perhaps she's waiting for us at the bus," said Mr. Coatsworth, as the few remaining passengers left the main deck.

"I bet she's been kidnapped!" Jessica hissed. "I knew he was the kidnapper all along. I bet he's tied her up and thrown her overboard."

"What about the doctor?" said Morgan. "He couldn't have thrown him overboard, he's twice his size."

"Oh!" shrieked Jessica, ignoring Morgan and digging her elbow into Avril. "Sharks!" She pointed to the grey sea. "They must have got the scent of blood when he dumped their battered

38

bodies into the sea!" She darted to the side of the ferry and peered into the murky water.

"I don't see no bodies," said Avril.

"Perhaps they've eaten them already," Jessica whispered in awe.

"They're not sharks," said Matthew. "They're porpoises."

Mr. Jones sighed wearily.

"Jessica," he said, "I don't think poor Miss Parker's body is floating in the sea. I don't think she's been eaten by sharks either. I think it's more likely she'll be waiting at the bus, as Mr. Coatsworth suggested. So why don't we go and see?"

39

The children followed Mr. Jones and Mr. Coatsworth down to the car deck. They passed the French car on the way to the bus, but it was empty.

Morgan and Sacha would have liked to have a good look at it, but didn't dare with Mr. Jones right in front of them.

"She's not here," said Jessica with satisfaction as they reached the bus. "I knew she wouldn't be."

"I hope she hasn't got lost," said Mr. Coatsworth, ushering the children onto the bus as the lorry at the front of the line started up its engine.

Mr. Jones leaned out of the door, glancing anxiously up and down the rows of vehicles. "Here she comes!" he cried, waving a map at the dishevelled figure that was running towards them.

"Oh my!" the French teacher murmured breathlessly as Mr. Jones helped her onto the bus. "I am so sorry to keep you waiting, but that poor old gentleman was so very upset. It took many glasses of cognac to calm down his nerves. It was fortunate that nice doctor was there to help," she added softly, smiling into a mirror and sticking one of her eyelashes back on.

Mr. Coatsworth's nostrils quivered expectantly

when she took a huge bottle of perfume from her bag and sprayed it vigorously behind her ears.

"And how are you feeling?" he murmured, putting the bus into first gear, and edging it forward.

A driver in the car lane next to them hooted his horn, drowning Miss Parker's reply. Another car hooted, then another. Then all the drivers in the lane were pressing their horns.

"What on earth is going on?" Mr. Jones shouted above the noise. "Why aren't they moving?"

The children crowded to the back window for a better view.

"There's a car without a driver holding them up," Matthew yelled. Morgan craned his neck to look. "It's that French car," he shouted, just as the bearded man who had been following them ran into view. He climbed into the car, shrugging his shoulders at the shaking fists of the other drivers, and started up the engine.

"Strange," Morgan murmured, as the children returned to their own seats. But what was much stranger was the figure of the other bearded man, lying bound and gagged in a lifeboat.

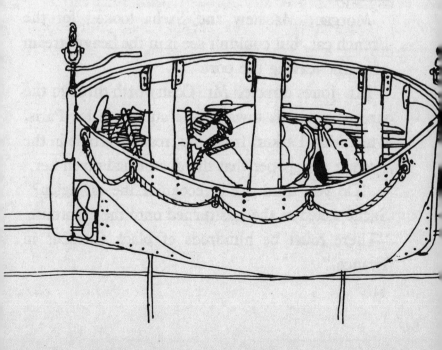

# 6
# The Arrival

Mr. Jones let Miss Parker handle the passports as her French was so much better than his, but the French official, seeing a bus full of English schoolchildren, merely glanced at the passports, handed them back to Miss Parker, and waved the bus through.

Morgan, Matthew and Sacha looked for the French car, but couldn't see it in the heavy stream of traffic leaving the port.

Mr. Jones directed Mr. Coatsworth through the streets of Calais towards the autoroute for Paris, while Miss Parker, frowning, read an article in the French newspaper that the doctor had given her.

"Do you think we'll recognize the car again?" Sacha asked as the bus turned onto the autoroute. "There must be hundreds of black Citroëns in France."

"16 90 75," Morgan said, producing a piece of paper from his pocket. "I wrote the number down."

16 90 75

Matthew, who was gazing out at the road, blinked. "Hey!" he said. "Isn't that the doctor?"

Morgan and Sacha turned to look out of the back window.

"Yes," said Morgan, watching the big American car pull out and overtake them. "I expect he's going to Paris too."

"M-Morgan," stuttered Sacha.

"Crikey!" shouted Morgan.

Roaring up behind them was a black Citroën.

"16 90 75!" Matthew yelled. "He's following us

again! Oh!" he added, perplexed, as the car overtook them, and raced up the autoroute. They watched it until it was only a speck in the distance. Matthew and Sacha sank back in their seats, disappointed.

"So he wasn't following us after all," muttered Sacha.

"I could have sworn he was," said Matthew, "the way he came tearing up behind us."

"Perhaps," said Morgan thoughtfully, "he wasn't following us in the first place.

"Perhaps," Morgan said again, "he was following someone else, and we just thought he was following us." He frowned. "Sacha!" he added excitedly. "Do you remember in Hampstead when I said it was a coincidence that a car with Paris number plates was behind us? Well, there was a taxi in front of it."

Sacha nodded.

"And on the motorway," Morgan continued, "before the French car overtook us, do you remember the taxi overtaking us?"

Sacha nodded again.

"Don't you see?" cried Morgan. "The Citroën wasn't following us, it was following the taxi. It was the taxi," he added breathlessly, "that was following us!"

"But why?" asked Matthew.

"I don't know," Morgan admitted.

Sacha thought for a moment. "But the taxi didn't follow us all the way to the ferry," he said. "How did he know we'd be on it?"

"When the bus pulled into the ferry lane," said Morgan, "it must have been obvious."

"So whoever was in the taxi was probably on the ferry too," murmured Matthew, "but then why was the man from the Citroën watching us through binoculars?"

"Perhaps it wasn't us he was watching," said Morgan. "Perhaps he was looking for the person that was in the taxi." He sighed. "I wish I knew who it was." Suddenly he whistled. "On the boat!" he cried. "When Miss Parker and the doctor took the other bearded man to the bar, he started to follow them."

"Of course," said Matthew, "but he ran away when he realized we'd seen him."

"In that case," said Morgan, "he must have been after the other bearded man, Miss Parker, or—" he paused, "the doctor." He whistled again. "The doctor. It must have been the doctor!" He glanced out of the window. "And he's following him right now!"

"Yes," said Sacha. "That must be it." He frowned. "I wonder why?"

"What I'm trying to work out," said Morgan, "is not why he's following the doctor, but why the doctor was following us."

The three boys sat silent in the back seat with puzzled expressions on their faces as the bus left the autoroute and drove through the sprawling outskirts of Paris. It wasn't until the bus entered the wide avenue leading to the Boulevard Madeleine that they jumped up and joined the rest of Class 3, who were shouting and waving at the people sitting in the pavement cafés.

# 7
# The Doctor Turns Up

Miss Parker pushed open the glass door and the children streamed into the hotel, while Mr. Coatsworth and Mr. Jones unloaded the luggage from the bus.

"Cor!" said Avril, gazing round the lobby in awe, not noticing the threadbare patches on the richly patterned carpets or the tarnish on the huge gilt mirrors or the chipped plaster on the decorative moulding that ran round the ceiling. Her eyes widened when she saw the ornate black metal cage next to the stairs.

"Golly!" she whispered. "What's that?"

Class 3 stared at the cage in alarm. A dreadful noise, like the wail of a banshee, poured from the darkness above it.

The chandeliers tinkled, rattles and groans filled the lobby as the children gazed spellbound, their

hands pressed against their ears, first at a pair of feet, then at a body, and finally at an anxious face that was peering at them through the panels, as the swaying lift descended slowly into the metal cage.

"What on earth is that terrible noise?" shouted Mr. Jones, rushing into the lobby, past the woman who was sitting unconcerned behind the reception desk.

"Oh," said Jessica in relief, "it's only the lift."

The metal gates clanged open and the manager of the hotel darted towards them, his arms outstretched. "*Bonjour, bonjour, Mademoiselle, Monsieur, mes enfants*," he cried, nodding at Miss Parker, Mr. Jones and the children. "Welcome," he added proudly. "My English is good, no? I work in London six months ago for five years."

The woman at the desk spoke sharply to him in French.

"Ah!" he corrected himself. "I work five years ago in London for six months. In a very posh hotel," he added, glancing forlornly at the exotic but shabby furniture in the lobby. "Five-star," he murmured sadly.

The woman sniffed and said quite clearly, "One."

The children, fascinated by the lift, had gone over to study it. Miss Parker tapped her foot impatiently, as the manager leaped over to where the woman sat and started shouting.

Miss Parker took a deep breath. *"Pourrais-je voir la chambre?"* she interrupted. *"S'il vous plaît."*

*"Pardon, pardon, Mademoiselle!"* The manager mopped his face with a handkerchief and trotted back to Miss Parker and Mr. Jones.

"My wife," he whispered, as the woman glared at him, "is a very excitable woman." He took a box of pills from his pocket and swallowed one. "And now to show you to your rooms."

By the time the children had taken turns going up and down in the lift, and decided which rooms they would have, it was nearly time for supper.

Mr. Jones told everyone to meet in the restaurant at seven o'clock, which gave them half an hour to unpack and tidy themselves up a bit.

Matthew, Morgan and Sacha, having decided to have the double room with an extra bed in it, heard the crash when Avril (who was sharing the room next door with Jessica) slammed the door behind her and, clutching her bottle of tomato ketchup, made her way down to the restaurant.

"Seven o'clock," said Matthew, "time for supper."

The boys left their room and pressed the button for the lift. They heard the noise of the lift coming down from the floor above, then six pairs of legs came into view.

"It's full," said Matthew. "Let's walk."

"Look!" hissed Morgan, pointing at the swaying lift.

"Crikey!" whispered Matthew, as it creaked slowly past them.

"Blimey!" murmured Sacha.

"The doctor!" Morgan breathed.

# 8
# The New Waiter

"Do you think we should tell Mr. Jones that the doctor's following us?" Sacha asked breathlessly, as they raced down the stairs.

"No," said Morgan, seeing the doctor step out of the lift into the lobby, "we've got to find out why first."

"I expect we'll find out soon," said Matthew, watching the doctor enter the restaurant. "Come on."

Mr. Jones was already sitting at a table with half the class. Mr. Coatsworth and Miss Parker sat at the next table with the rest of the children.

"Look who's here!" Matthew hissed.

"Good heavens!" cried Mr. Jones, jumping up and holding his hand out in greeting when he recognized the doctor. "What an amazing coincidence!" He winced, as the grinning doctor

crushed his hand and nodded to Miss Parker and Mr. Coatsworth.

"Are you staying at the hotel?" Mr. Jones added, rubbing his knuckles, but the doctor only frowned and looked inquiringly at Miss Parker who spoke rapidly in French. The doctor grinned again, holding up three stubby fingers.

"He's staying for three days," said Miss Parker.

"Would you care to join us for dinner?" Mr. Jones asked politely, as the children stared at the doctor. Miss Parker spoke to him again, and the doctor nodded.

"Jolly good," said Mr. Jones, waving to the manager.

The manager seemed even more excited than usual as he ran over to them with an extra chair. "I have a new waiter tonight," he hissed in Mr. Jones's ear. He winced at the sound of crashing dishes from the kitchen. "Very new," he added, handing the elaborate menus around the two tables.

The new waiter, a strange-looking fellow with a long droopy moustache, hovered by them, knocking over Avril's bottle of ketchup every time he darted forward to brush crumbs off the table-cloth where the doctor was sitting.

Avril and Jessica decided to have fish and chips, but it took the rest of the children a long time to decide what to eat, there were so many things to choose from.

"It's an incredible menu for such a small hotel," said Mr. Jones.

"Incredible," he repeated as the waiter charged towards them, clutching two plates of fish and chips.

The manager, who was following the waiter, stooped to pick up the sprigs of parsley that fell to the floor as the waiter dropped the hot plates onto the table.

"I was just saying," said Mr. Jones, as the waiter mopped up the glass of water he'd knocked over and the manager arranged the parsley on the plates, "what an incredible menu you have!" He looked around at the other, empty tables. "I'm surprised the restaurant isn't crowded."

The manager beamed, and clasped his hands together. "Ah yes." He sighed, taking the menu from Mr. Jones and gazing at it with misty eyes. "This is the same menu as in my five-star Mayfair hotel." He kissed his fingers.

"*Très bon!*" He handed the menu back to Mr. Jones. "Unfortunately, though, the suckling pig in cherry sauce, which you so wisely chose, is off!"

"Never mind," said Mr. Jones cheerfully. "I'll have the same as Mr. Coatsworth and Miss Parker, the rack of lamb with rosemary and button mushrooms."

"Ah!" cried the manager. "Lamb with rosemary and button mushrooms. Beautiful. But sadly, that is off too."

"How about the chicken breasts stuffed with garlic butter?" said Mr. Coatsworth.

"With tiny baby marrows?" exclaimed the

manager, as Mr. Coatsworth nodded enthusiastically. "Wonderful, wonderful! But," he added regretfully, "I don't have it today."

Mr. Jones glanced at the menu again. "Steak in red wine?" he asked hopefully. "Veal in cream with truffles?" he added, as the manager shook his head. "Pike in lobster sauce? Trout with almonds?" he asked in desperation.

"You have wonderful taste," said the manager gravely. "You would have liked my five-star hotel. There I had the pike and trouts in almonds."

"What have you got?" asked Mr. Coatsworth.

"Fish and chips," said the manager.

"That will do," said Mr. Jones wearily, handing the menu back to him. "It's the best meal I've ever listened to," he added.

"I think," said Miss Parker, who was watching Avril in dismay as she poured half a bottle of ketchup over her fish and chips, "I will have only a piece of cheese and a glass of red wine."

"I thought you liked fish and chips," said Mr. Coatsworth in surprise.

"Oh I do!" she cried. "I adore chips and fish." She looked at Avril's plate again and shuddered.

"But I don't feel too hungry right now."

Jessica, who had finished her fish and chips and was still starving, picked up a menu to see what the puddings were. "I don't see fish anywhere," she said, showing the menu to Mr. Jones.

"There," said Mr. Jones, pointing.

The waiter, with the manager following anxiously behind, was on his third trip from the kitchen when Jessica screamed.

"I've been poisoned!" she cried, sliding down her seat and clutching her stomach.

The bottle of wine the waiter was carrying slipped through his fingers and crashed to the floor as he gazed at her in horror.

"The fish," Jessica's faint voice wafted up from under the table.

"It's poisoned!"

"Don't be daft," said Avril, stepping over her body to get to the bottle of ketchup.

"It said so!" Jessica continued indignantly, pulling herself up to show Avril. "On the menu— look! And we've all eaten it!" Jessica shrieked, pointing dramatically to Miss Parker. "Except for her. I bet he's still after her," she continued wildly. "I bet the kidnapper followed her from the boat. I bet he knows she likes fish and chips. That's why he poisoned the fish! He thought he'd get her! But he got us instead!"

"*Poisson*," said Mr. Jones gently, as the rest of the children looked at one another in alarm, "means fish in French."

"Oh," said Jessica, "are you sure?"

"Quite," said Mr. Jones.

"Well, at least he didn't get us this time," she added darkly.

Miss Parker's eyes narrowed as she gazed at Jessica.

"You have a very vivid imagination, child," she said.

Morgan, Matthew and Sacha watched every movement as the doctor (with the waiter hovering at his side, mopping up spilled wine and dropping crumbs into the glass as he offered more bread) finished his meal.

"Well," said Mr. Jones, as the doctor glanced at his watch and stood up, "it was very nice seeing you. I expect we'll bump into you again."

The doctor handed a bundle of francs to the waiter, grinned at everyone, then pulling a gold toothpick from his pocket, sauntered out of the restaurant.

Matthew, Morgan and Sacha looked at one another in dismay.

"Excuse me!" Morgan shouted, jumping up and running out of the restaurant. "I need to go to the toilet," he called over his shoulder to the startled

children. The waiter, having glanced at the money in his hand, hesitated, and ran out after him.

The doctor was pushing open the glass doors when Morgan saw him, but by the time he had followed him outside, he was already stepping into a taxi. He heard the word *"château"* being shouted at the driver, but the noise of the traffic drowned the rest of the words. Morgan turned to go back into the hotel when the taxi disappeared round a corner, and collided with the waiter, who was on his way out.

"Sorry," said Morgan, but the waiter didn't seem to hear him—he was gazing up and down the road, frowning. Morgan frowned too. Something about the waiter's expression seemed vaguely familiar to him.

"Haven't I seen you somewhere before?" he asked.

The waiter looked startled. "Me? *Non!* I have many brothers," he said, turning abruptly and going back into the hotel. Morgan followed, still frowning, into the restaurant.

Miss Parker had already gone to bed and Mr. Jones told the children that as it was nearly ten o'clock, they should go to bed too.

"Did you see where he went?" Matthew asked, when all the children, having said good night to one another, were making their way to their rooms.

"He got into a taxi," Morgan replied. "I heard the word *château*, but that was all."

"There must be hundreds of *châteaux* around Paris," said Sacha, as the three boys stepped into the lift.

"That waiter," said Morgan, unlocking their door. "I'm sure I've seen him before." He sighed and shook his head. "There's so many strange things going on. I'm beginning to be suspicious of everyone."

The boys talked until midnight, then exhausted, they fell asleep.

It was Jessica's piercing scream that woke them up.

# 9
# Ghosts!

The door of Jessica and Avril's room was thrown open and Jessica, looking like Lady Macbeth in her white nightie, was framed in the doorway. She was shrieking at the top of her voice. One by one the doors in the corridor were cautiously opened and pale, anxious faces peered from behind them.

"What's wrong?" shouted Morgan, running from his room, followed by Sacha and Matthew.

"I've just seen a ghost!" screeched Jessica.

"Rhubarb!" Avril's muffled voice drifted from the darkened room where she was lying with a pillow pressed over her head, trying to get back to sleep.

"It was *horrible!*" Jessica continued wildly, ignoring Avril, as the rest of Class 3, realizing it was Jessica making all the noise, gathered round her.

She clutched her forehead and shuddered. "*Horrible!*" she repeated.

The screams had woken Mr. Jones, whose room was above Jessica's. Jessica, seeing Mr. Jones running down the stairs, shrieked again, waking the manager and his wife, whose rooms were above Mr. Jones's.

"What on earth is going on?" Mr. Jones demanded.

"Jessica says she's seen a ghost," said Matthew,

as Morgan bent down to pick up something from the floor.

"I didn't see no ghost," Avril retorted.

"You might not have, but I did," Jessica shouted back. "And I heard it coming too."

"First I heard the rattle of chains," she whispered. "Then I heard unearthly moans as it dragged itself along the corridor, then the door creaked open ever so slowly." She paused, looking at the wide-eyed children.

"Then," she hissed, "this white thing, simply covered in bloodstains, started floating round the room."

Mr. Jones sighed wearily. "Jessica," he said, "it was just a bad dream. It was probably the noise of the lift that caused it," he added, as the lift, creaking and groaning, clanged to a standstill and the manager leaped out.

"Is anything wrong?" he asked, wringing his hands.

"No," said Mr. Jones firmly, patting Jessica on the head as she opened her mouth to speak. "Jessica has just had a bad dream. She's had a lot of excitement today," he added, frowning.

"*Oui, oui,*" the manager muttered. "We all

have. Too much. Too much," he repeated, sighing deeply.

"Perhaps it was the noise from the lift," he suggested. "Perhaps the young lady would rather move to Room 6? It's not so noisy there. *Ah non!*" He shook his head. "Stupid me! I forgot. Room 6 is taken."

"She's already in Room 6," said Akbar, pointing at the number on the door.

"No I'm not," said Jessica, "I'm in Room 9."

70

"Then why does it say 6?" Akbar demanded.

"The room number must have slipped when you slammed the door at supper time," said Matthew.

"I didn't slam the door," said Jessica. "It was Avril going back for her tomato ketchup."

The manager looked at the door in alarm.

"I'll have the number screwed back properly," he said, glancing down the corridor. "In the morning."

"And now," said Mr. Jones briskly when Jessica, having decided she wanted to stay in Room 9 anyway, had calmed down sufficiently to go back to bed, "everyone back to their own room."

Matthew yawned as he, Morgan and Sacha returned to their room.

"Jessica's always imagining things," he said.

"A ghost, covered in bloodstains, floating round the room," said Sacha in a quavering voice, dipping his shoulders and pretending to fly.

"Bloodstains," Morgan murmured, unclenching his fist and gazing at the silver button in his hand.

"*Bloodstains!*" he shouted, waving the button at Matthew and Sacha.

"Y-you don't think she really saw a ghost?" Matthew stuttered in surprise, gazing blankly at the button.

"Not a ghost," said Morgan grimly. "But a wine-stained waiter! And this," he added excitedly, as Matthew and Sacha stared at him in disbelief, "is one of his jacket buttons!"

"I suppose," said Sacha slowly, "that with his black trousers in a dark room, his white jacket would seem to be floating."

"And the noise," whispered Matthew, "was the noise of the lift when he came up!"

Sacha frowned. "But what would he want in Jessica and Avril's room?" he asked. Morgan, who had sat down on his bed to think, jumped up.

"The room number!" he cried. "That's it! He didn't mean to go into their room at all! He meant to go into Room 6!"

"Do you think we ought to tell Mr. Jones?" Sacha asked.

"No," said Morgan, climbing into bed. "Not yet. First we have to find out who's in Room 6. And I wouldn't be at all surprised," he added, switching off his bedside lamp, "if it happened to be the doctor's room! But what I really wish I knew," he said, closing his eyes, "is why that waiter looked so familiar."

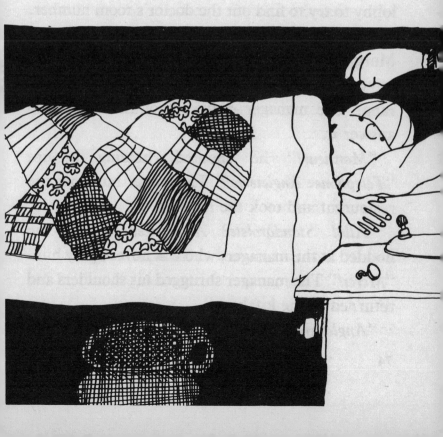

# 10
# The Waiter's Trip

Morgan, Matthew and Sacha woke up early the next morning. They dressed quickly, then, using the stairs as the lift was so noisy, crept down to the lobby to try to find out the doctor's room number.

"Perhaps it's in the guest book," whispered Morgan, nodding towards the reception desk. "Oh crikey!" he added, as the telephone on the desk rang. The manager came out of the kitchen to answer it.

"*Monsieur!*" he shouted, holding it up. "*Téléphone. Angleterre!*" The waiter ran from the restaurant and took the receiver.

"*Allô! Standaroiste? Angleterre? Merci!*" he nodded at the manager, who was hovering by him. "*Merci!*" The manager shrugged his shoulders and returned to the kitchen.

"*Angleterre!*" hissed Sacha, as the three boys

pressed against the side of the stairs hidden from the waiter. "That's England!"

The waiter was speaking in halting English. "Good!" he said. "Nine o'clock?" He glanced at his watch.

"Arriving Calais ten thirty? Excellent. I should just make it. *Merci, Monsieur*." He smiled as he replaced the receiver. Then, picking it up again, he dialled a number.

"What's he saying?" Morgan asked Sacha, as the waiter spoke rapidly in French. Sacha frowned, concentrating. "I can't understand much of it," he replied, "but it's something about the doctor. It sounds like 'forget about the doctor, the other one has turned up.' " He frowned again. " 'I think the doctor is clean,' " he finished, as the waiter put the receiver back.

" 'I think the doctor is clean,' " Morgan repeated, as the manager reappeared. "What can that mean?"

"Sssh!" said Sacha, craning his head forward.

The manager and the waiter were talking quietly together.

"What did they say?" Matthew asked, as the boy Henri appeared, carrying a coat which he handed to the waiter before slipping into the white jacket the waiter had taken off.

"He just thanked him a lot," said Sacha, bewildered. "And something about his services not being needed any more!"

"He must have fired him," said Morgan.

"I'm not surprised," muttered Matthew.

"No," said Sacha, shaking his head. "The manager didn't say that to the waiter. The waiter said that to the manager."

"Are you sure?" Morgan asked, perplexed.

"That's what it sounded like to me," said Sacha.

"Things are getting weirder and weirder." Morgan sighed.

"They've gone now," said Matthew, watching the waiter leaving through the glass doors and the manager and Henri returning to the kitchen again. "Now to find out if the doctor's room number is in the book."

"Wait!" said Morgan, pulling Matthew back as the lift started rumbling. "Someone's coming!"

"Talk of the devil!" Sacha murmured as the lift door clanged open and the doctor stepped out.

The boys looked at one another as the doctor tossed his key on the reception desk and strolled into the restaurant.

"We'll find out for certain now!" cried Morgan, darting down the few remaining stairs, followed by Matthew and Sacha. "It's 6 all right," he said, glancing at the number on the key.

"That means," said Matthew, "that he's being followed by two people. The bearded man in the Citroën and the waiter."

"Except the bearded man seems to have disappeared," said Sacha.

"And now the waiter's gone too," added Morgan. "To Calais. I wonder why?"

"Perhaps we ought to tell Mr. Jones," suggested Sacha.

"Tell him what?" demanded Matthew. "That the doctor followed us to the ferry in a taxi? That the bearded man in the Citroën was following the doctor who was following us? That the bearded man has disappeared and the waiter has started following the doctor instead?" He paused for breath. "And that the waiter broke into the doctor's room in the middle of the night, only it wasn't the doctor's room after all, it was Avril and Jessica's? And anyway he isn't following the doctor any more because he's gone to Calais." He shook his head. "It doesn't make sense. He'd never believe us!"

"Especially after all that trouble with the other bearded man on the boat," said Morgan thoughtfully. "Perhaps we'd better not tell him." He paused as the noise of the lift drowned his words. "Not yet, anyway," he added, as Jessica and Avril (clutching her bottle of tomato ketchup) stepped out of the lift. "Come on. We could spend all day trying to work it out. Let's go in for breakfast. I'm hungry."

The three boys went into the restaurant and sat down, followed by Jessica and Avril.

They watched the doctor closely, as the rest of Class 3 drifted in noisily discussing Jessica's ghost. Mr. Jones came through the door with a sleepy-looking Mr. Coatsworth trailing behind him.

"Good morning," he said brightly, smiling at the doctor before glancing round the tables where the children were sitting. "I hope you all slept well," he added, his eyes resting on Jessica.

"Huh. Some hopes!" snorted Avril.

The door swung open again and Miss Parker walked in. She nodded to the doctor as she approached the table that Avril was sitting at. Then, noticing the sticky bottle of tomato ketchup, she changed direction and sat at the end of the other table.

"I hope the noise didn't disturb you last night?" Mr. Jones said. Miss Parker shook her head. "I did not hear any noise," she replied. "I slept like a branch."

"What noise?" asked Mr. Coatsworth, who had slept like a log.

"Jessica had a bad dream," said Mr. Jones, picking the huge breakfast menu up from the table and glancing at it. Then, remembering the supper the night before, he quickly put it down again.

"No, I didn't," said Jessica stoutly. "I saw a ghost."

"We'll have to tell Jessica about the waiter," Morgan whispered to Sacha and Matthew. "It's not fair!"

"Later!" hissed Sacha, jerking his head towards the doctor. "When he's not around."

"Well!" said Mr. Jones. "Let's forget about ghosts and order our breakfast. We won't want to be late setting off. We've got a lot to see today."

The manager bustled in carrying more menus and smiling at the children, followed by Henri carrying a tray of rolls and a large pot of coffee.

"*Bonjour, bonjour!*" cried the manager. "Would you like to look at my wonderful menus?"

"I don't think so," said Mr. Jones doubtfully. "Perhaps you'd better tell us what you've got."

"Oh!" said the manager, disappointed. "A pity." He paused and studied the menu, as Henri banged the tray down in front of Mr. Jones.

"At my five-star hotel I had kidneys, three different types of fish, eggs—boiled, scrambled, fried—mushrooms, tomatoes, sausages . . ." His wife shouted angrily from the kitchen, interrupting him. *"Pardon!"* he said, hurrying back to the kitchen. *"Bon appétit!"*

"I wish he wouldn't keep telling us what he hasn't got," muttered Avril, who had been looking forward to fried bread and sausages, smothered in ketchup.

"The French don't eat large breakfasts," said Mr. Jones, passing around the rolls to the hungry children.

"In this hotel", said Akbar, taking one, "they're lucky to eat at all!"

When the children had finished their breakfast, which didn't take long, Mr. Jones produced a typewritten sheet of paper from his pocket.

"The itinerary," he said, holding it up. "Monday morning the Eiffel Tower." He paused as the children cheered. "Then lunch. Monday afternoon a boat ride on the Seine, then a visit to Notre Dame."

"Where the Hunchback comes from," breathed Jessica, as the rest of the children cheered again.

"Tuesday," he continued, "morning, a stroll around Montmartre, taking in the Sacré Coeur, lunch. Afternoon, the Louvre. Wednesday," he went on, "all day at Versailles. Thursday morning a bit of shopping, lunch, then back to Calais for the five o'clock ferry."

The manager, who had reappeared and was standing behind Mr. Jones suddenly frowned. "*Ah, non!*" he cried, shaking his head and pointing at the paper. "The Louvre is closed on Tuesdays."

"Impossible!" cried Miss Parker, choking on the coffee she was drinking. "It can't be," she gasped as Mr. Coatsworth thumped her on her back.

"Ah! But I'm afraid it is so," said the manager in surprise. "It is always closed on Tuesdays."

"We'll just have to do a bit of swapping

around," said Mr. Jones, looking at the itinerary again. "We can't miss the Louvre." He glanced at Miss Parker, who was still looking agitated, as Mr. Coatsworth mopped up the coffee that she'd spilled. "We'll go this afternoon," he added, "and do the boat trip tomorrow."

Miss Parker bit her lip. "I think as I will be walking a lot this afternoon I had better miss the Eiffel Tower this morning." She looked down at her bandaged leg. "I did not get too much sleep with my leg last night."

"Perhaps the doctor would have a look at it for

you," suggested Mr. Coatsworth in concern.

Miss Parker looked startled, then she smiled. "Ah, yes! Of course, the doctor." She glanced over to where the doctor was sitting. "I shall ask him," she murmured.

"And then why not have a rest in your room?" said Mr. Jones, standing up. "I'm sure Mr. Coatsworth wouldn't mind helping me keep an eye on the children." Mr. Coatsworth nodded, hoping Mr. Jones didn't expect him to go to the top of the Tower with them as he didn't have a head for heights.

"So we'll meet you at three o'clock at the main entrance to the Louvre," said Mr. Coatsworth. "If your leg is better."

"It's such a lovely day," said Mr. Jones as they stepped out into the brilliant sunshine. "Why don't we walk? It's not far from here."

"Fine," said Mr. Coatsworth, as half the class, having spotted the Tower in the distance, were already heading in that direction anyway.

"Come on, you lot!" Mr. Jones shouted, looking back at Morgan, Matthew and Sacha, who were still standing by the glass doors, staring into the hotel.

"It's a pity about Miss Parker's leg," said Mr. Coatsworth, as the three boys caught up with him and Mr. Jones.

"I expect she'll feel better after a rest," said Mr. Jones. "She's in good hands."

"But is she?" Sacha muttered to Morgan.

"Is she what?" asked Morgan vaguely.

"In good hands," Sacha repeated. "What's wrong with you?" he demanded, when Morgan didn't reply.

Morgan frowned. "Miss Parker," he said. "She said she didn't get much sleep with her leg. But earlier she said she'd slept like a log, or rather a branch," he corrected himself.

# 11
# The Eiffel Tower

They walked along the Rue Royale, through the Place de la Concorde, and when the children stopped on the Concorde bridge to wave at the boats crowded with tourists going up the Seine, Mr. Jones told them the bridge was made from stones taken from the Bastille.

The children became more and more excited as the huge iron girders of the Eiffel Tower loomed closer and closer. Even Matthew, Morgan and Sacha, who had been discussing the strange events at the hotel, stopped talking and gazed at it in awe.

"It's fantastic," said Morgan, shielding his eyes against the sun as he stopped to look up at the summit. "Come on!" he added to Matthew and Sacha, who had stopped to admire it too. Then, pulling them along with him, he started running towards the monument.

The children stood under the Tower and gazed up in wonder at the lacy framework.

"What an amazing piece of engineering," Mr. Jones said, when he and Mr. Coatsworth had caught up with them. "Did you know that three hundred men were employed to build it?"

"I wonder how many were left when it was finished," murmured Mr. Coatsworth.

Mr. Jones smiled. "The incredible thing is, not one of them fell. They were chosen especially for their agility. It must have been like watching three hundred acrobats! Incredible!" he repeated, not noticing Jessica who, spotting a group of people and wanting to know what the French guide was showing them, had slipped away.

"Two million five hundred thousand rivets were used," Mr. Jones continued, "and the height can vary up to six inches, depending on the weather." He paused, as Jessica, squealing with excitement, came running towards him.

"Someone did fall!" she cried, pointing to where the guide had been standing. "And he's buried there!"

"Who fell?" asked Mr. Jones, as Jessica dragged

A.G. EIFFEL
1832 · 1923

him towards the spot, followed by Mr. Coatsworth
and the rest of Class 3.

"Eiffel!" Jessica pointed to a bronze plaque.
"He fell. The French guide said so!"

"Poor devil," muttered Mr. Coatsworth.

"Oh!" Jessica added, shuddering. "Perhaps it
was his ghost I saw last night!"

"Jessica," said Mr. Jones, "Eiffel is pronounced
Eefell in French. The guide didn't say 'He fell,' he
said 'Eefell'. He wasn't showing anyone Eiffel's
tombstone, he was showing them his plaque."

"Maybe it was his ghost I saw last night," Avril
repeated sarcastically as the children studied the
plaque, while Mr. Jones, followed by Mr. Coatsworth who was looking rather nervous, joined the
line for tickets into the Tower. She dug Jessica
with her elbow. "I keep telling you, you didn't see
no ghost. There ain't such things. It's all in your
imagination."

"She did see something," Morgan interrupted,
"but it wasn't a ghost."

90

The children listened open-mouthed as he, Sacha and Matthew told them about the button, the room number and the telephone conversations.

Jessica wanted to tell Mr. Jones, but the rest of the children persuaded her not to until they'd discovered just what the doctor was up to.

Akbar was all for sneaking back to the hotel to spy on the doctor, but changed his mind when he saw Mr. Jones coming towards them holding entrance tickets to the Tower. Mr. Coatsworth was trailing behind him, eyeing the monument apprehensively.

"I thought you'd want to go right to the top," said Mr. Jones cheerfully as Mr. Coatsworth winced. "It's such a clear day, the view should be magnificent." Class 3 followed Mr. Jones up the stairs to the lift, overtaking Mr. Coatsworth who was lagging behind.

"Come on, Mr. Coatsworth," Avril shouted as Mr. Jones ushered the children into the lift.

Mr. Coatsworth reluctantly stepped forward and into the lift. He clung to the side of it, his eyes tightly closed, as the metal cage slowly rose upward.

The roar of the traffic melted away as the lift

ascended, and soon the children were looking down at rooftops, and then at the Seine and the tiny boats dotted along it drifting under the bridges.

"Isn't it wonderful?" Jessica sighed, shaking Mr. Coatsworth's arm.

Mr. Coatsworth cautiously opened one eye. "Wonderful," he murmured, then quickly closed the eye.

"I wonder how many bodies are floating down it," Jessica said thoughtfully.

"Here we are!" said Mr. Jones as the lift swayed, then came to a standstill. Mr. Coatsworth sighed in relief as they got out, but his face fell when he saw Mr. Jones heading towards another lift.

"Now to the top," said Mr. Jones, as Class 3 trooped into the lift. "This is where the view really gets magnificent."

"It's looking a bit full," said Mr. Coatsworth. "Perhaps I'd better wait here for you."

"It ain't full," said Avril, tugging at his arm. "There's stacks of room." And catching him off balance, she dragged him into the lift.

"Just think," said Mr. Jones as the lift stopped and the children surged out onto the top platform, "we're now eight hundred and ninety-eight feet above the ground."

Mr. Coatsworth groaned, and closed his eyes again as the children crowded to the edge of the Tower and gazed in awe at Paris, which was spread out before them like a huge map.

"The oscillation at the top," continued Mr.

Jones, "never exceeds five inches."

"Please, sir," said Akbar, "what does oscillation mean?"

"If something is oscillating," Mr. Jones replied, "it means it's swaying. Well, as I was saying, the bit right at the top there never oscillates more than five inches, even in a gale."

"Sir," said Matthew, glancing at Mr. Coatsworth who had turned very pale. "Mr. Coatsworth is . . ."

"Is what?" Mr. Jones asked, gazing at the summit.

"Oscillating more than five inches," said Matthew.

"Oh dear," said Mr. Jones in concern, as Mr. Coatsworth sank slowly onto a bench. "Are you all right?"

Mr. Coatsworth smiled weakly. "I don't have much of a head for heights," he replied, licking his dry lips. "My mouth's a bit parched, that's all."

"I'll get you a strong cup of coffee," said Mr. Jones, noticing a refreshment stand behind them. "That should put you right."

Mr. Coatsworth stared straight ahead with

glazed eyes, hardly daring to drink the coffee that Mr. Jones had given him in case the slightest movement should bring the Tower toppling down. Declining the invitation to go to the summit, he sat bolt upright, waiting, while Mr. Jones took the children up the stairs to show them the room where Eiffel himself had lived.

"Well," said Mr. Jones, glancing at his watch as he came back down the stairs, followed by the children, "one thirty already. Would you believe it? Time flies when you're enjoying yourself."

Mr. Coatsworth risked a gloomy nod.

"We'd better go and have some lunch if we're to be at the Louvre by three," Mr. Jones continued. "We don't want to keep Miss Parker waiting. We could go to that little place just by the entrance to the Tower," he added. "It looked quite pleasant."

The children didn't want to leave, but as they were feeling hungry, they followed him to the lifts.

Mr. Coatsworth, keeping well away from the edge, carefully inched his way behind them. The first lift wasn't crowded, but when they got out at the second stage, to get the lift to the first stage, there was quite a queue. Morgan, who wanted to see the lift arriving, climbed onto the handrail so he could see over the heads of the people in front.

"Crikey!" he exclaimed, waving at two figures at the front of the line. "It's Polly and Peter!"

"Who are they?" Sacha asked, seeing the figures turn and wave back.

"Polly and Peter Oxley," Morgan replied. "They live in my street. They must be on holiday," he added as the lift arrived, the doors opened and Polly and Peter stepped in, still waving.

"We thought you'd be here," Polly shouted, squeezing to the front of the lift which was gradually filling up, "when we saw your head-mistress."

"Where? In the hospital?" Morgan shouted back in surprise, as Class 3 edged closer to the lift. A uniformed man stepped forward just as Polly replied and, speaking to Mr. Jones in French, hooked a rope in front of them.

"Friends of yours, Morgan?" Mr. Jones asked, not hearing Polly's reply as he'd been listening to the French guard telling them to wait for the next lift as that one was full.

"Yes, sir," said Morgan slowly. "And they just said they'd seen Miss Barker."

"Really?" said Mr. Jones, as the lift gates shut. "In the hospital?"

"No," said Morgan. "In Paris."

# 12

# Bent on Revenge

"They must have been mistaken," Mr. Jones said as they sat in the pavement café eating their lunch. "They probably saw someone who looked like her. Miss Barker couldn't possibly be in Paris."

"How do they know her anyway?" Matthew asked.

"Their mother and Miss Barker are old school friends," Morgan replied, gazing at the crowd of people milling round the Tower, hoping to see Polly and Peter again. "They see a lot of her." He shook his head, ignoring Jessica, who kept punctuating the conversation with screams and groans, putting children with weak stomachs off their food as she vividly described a fiendish doctor's gruesome method of dealing with patients he didn't like.

"They must have seen someone who looked like Miss Barker," he agreed, frowning thoughtfully as Avril (having discovered the bottle of ketchup in her jacket pocket) calmly tipped it over her food at the same time that Jessica reached the gory climax of her story.

"Talking of Miss Barker," said Mr. Jones, "we mustn't forget we're meeting Miss Parker at three o'clock. I'll settle the bill, then we'd better be off." He signalled for the waiter, who was looking in dismay at all the half-eaten plates of food on Avril and Jessica's table.

"It was an excellent meal," said Mr. Jones, smiling at the waiter as he brought the bill.

"Goodness, what a surly fellow," he murmured, as the waiter sniffed disdainfully and stalked away.

Class 3 followed Mr. Jones and Mr. Coatsworth away from the restaurant. Morgan, who was still searching for Polly and Peter, turned to have one last look at the Tower's forecourt. He stopped and shielded his eyes against the sun.

"It can't be," he muttered.

"What's wrong?" asked Matthew, running back with Sacha to where Morgan was standing.

"Over there!" said Morgan pointing.

"The balloon seller?" asked Sacha.

"No," said Morgan. "In front of him."

Jessica, who had noticed the three boys gazing towards the Tower, ran back too.

"Oh!" she cried, her eyes widening when she saw the small figure stumbling towards them. She backed slowly away, then turned and raced off again.

"Come on!" Matthew whispered, nudging Morgan and Sacha, who were staring in amazement at the advancing figure. "Let's go!"

The man shouted hoarsely as the three boys ran to catch up with the rest of Class 3.

"What on earth is going on?" Mr. Jones demanded as Jessica, her finger pointing dramatically at the Eiffel Tower, collapsed to the ground.

"The kidnapper!" Jessica gasped, as the children clustered round her. "He's after us. Bent on revenge.

"I knew he was following us," she went on breathlessly, "when Miss Parker didn't have fish. I bet he's in league with the fiendish doctor." Her eyes narrowed as she looked at Mr. Jones's bewildered face.

"And the waiter," she hissed. "I bet they're all in league!"

"Jessica," said Mr. Jones, "you're imagining things. There's nobody after us . . ."

"Oh yes there is," cried Sacha, overhearing Mr. Jones as he, Morgan and Matthew ran towards the group of children. He pointed at the Eiffel Tower.

"That's only a balloon seller," said Mr. Jones.

"In front of him," said Sacha, pointing again.

"Good heavens!" said Mr. Jones. "It's the bearded man from the boat. The one you attacked," he added nervously, glancing at the children. "I wonder what he wants? He sounds terribly agitated."

"Do you think we ought to hang around to find out?" murmured Mr. Coatsworth.

"Perhaps not," Mr. Jones replied, remembering the state the man had been in after the attack.

"Anyway," he added quickly, noticing the children slipping off in the direction of the Métro, "we don't have time to chat."

"He's still coming," Mr. Coatsworth observed, glancing over his shoulder as he tried to keep up with Mr. Jones, who was striding after the children. "And a balloon seller seems to be coming too. He's catching up," he gasped, as Mr. Jones broke into a trot.

"Stop! Stop!" the man shouted, as he struggled

after them. "I want to ask you something!"

"He's carrying a bunch of flowers," Mr. Coatsworth said in surprise, slowing down.

"So he is," Mr. Jones, slowing down too as the man caught up with them.

The children saw the flowers and cautiously crept back towards Mr. Jones and Mr. Coatsworth.

"Goodness!" said Mr. Jones, turning to face the

breathless man. "What a coincidence! Fancy meeting you here. Can't stay," he added, looking at his watch.

"Wait!" the man gasped, clutching Mr. Jones's arm as he turned to go. "I've been trying to catch up with you for the last ten minutes."

"Have you?" asked Mr. Jones in a surprised voice. "We didn't notice." The man waved the bunch of flowers. "I saw you leaving the restaurant so I bought these to give to that nice teacher." His eyes darted round the group of children, looking for Miss Parker. "The one that was so kind to me on the boat."

"Oh," said Mr. Jones in relief. "She decided to stay at the hotel this morning. Her leg was bothering her."

"Which hotel?" the man asked quickly. "I'll deliver them personally. Just a little token, that's all."

"The Hôtel Groblin Madeleine," Mr. Jones replied.

"Thanks," said the man, dashing to the kerb.

"Oh dear," said Mr. Jones, as the man stepped into a taxi. "I should have told him she's probably left the hotel by now."

"Oh look!" cried Avril as a great cloud of multi-coloured balloons came bobbing towards them.

"How much?" she demanded, stepping in front of the legs that protruded from them. A pair of eyes peered between the balloons, then thrusting the whole bunch into Avril's hand, the man who had been holding them darted towards the road and hailed a taxi too.

"If that man had a moustache," said Morgan, catching a glimpse of the man's face as he ran from them, "he'd be the double of the waiter from the hotel."

"Yes," agreed Matthew.
"But it can't be him.
He went to Calais."
"Come on, children,"
Mr. Jones interrupted.
"Let's get to the Louvre."

# 13
# The Mona Lisa

They arrived at the Louvre at ten past three, but Miss Parker wasn't there.

"Perhaps she's gone in already," said Mr. Coatsworth as they stood on the steps of the main entrance.

"I don't know why we're bothering to wait," Jessica whispered to Avril, whose face was hidden by the balloons. "She won't be coming. I bet the kidnapper was too late. I bet the doctor has got rid of her body already." The balloons parted.

"Don't be daft," said Avril, gazing through the gap. "Here she comes now."

Jessica's eyes widened in disbelief when she saw Miss Parker hurrying towards them.

"I'm sorry I'm late a little," Miss Parker cried, running up the steps. "But that very kind doctor insisted on putting on my leg a fresh bandage."

"Oh, it's quite all right," said Mr. Jones. "We were rather late ourselves. We bumped into . . ."

"I'm sure you're very anxious to see all those wonderful paintings," Miss Parker interrupted, striding towards the entrance. "I am. I have never before clapped eyes on the *Mona Lisa*," she added. Mr. Jones and Mr. Coatsworth hurried after her, trying to ask her if the bearded man had called to see her at the hotel, but not getting a chance to as she strode ahead of them, chattering all the time.

"All my life for this moment I have waited," she continued, turning to count the children when she reached the ticket office. "Three adults and twenty children," she said, rapping the desk to attract the attention of the girl behind it; who was engrossed in a newspaper.

"*Pardon!*" said the girl, putting the newspaper down and hurriedly getting the tickets.

Morgan, who was at the end of the line of children, glanced idly at the newspaper on the desk. Noticing the date on it, he wondered why the girl was bothering to read a newspaper that was a day old. His eyes travelled down the columns of

type on the page, trying to work out what the girl found so interesting. He gasped when he saw the small photograph at the bottom of the page.

"Sacha!" he cried, pulling his friend back. "Look!"

"Crikey!" exclaimed Sacha, gazing at the photograph. "It's the bearded man. The one we've just seen!"

"What does it say?" Morgan asked urgently, as Mr. Jones shouted at them to hurry up.

"Something about paintings," murmured Sacha, frowning with concentration as he bent over the newspaper.

*"Pardon!"* The girl behind the desk smiled at them, nodded towards Mr. Jones, who was beckoning to them, and picked up the newspaper.

Morgan and Sacha groaned as they ran to catch up with the rest of Class 3. Miss Parker, already half-way up a flight of stairs, stopped to wait for Mr. Jones and Mr. Coatsworth, struggling behind her.

"Did you see the old gentleman from the boat?" Mr. Jones asked as she pointed to a sign.

"The *Mona Lisa* this way is," she said, not hearing Mr. Jones. "Come on!" she added, frowning at the group of children who had stopped to admire a huge painting of a battle scene.

Morgan and Sacha, having quickly told Matthew about the photograph in the newspaper, left him to tell the rest of Class 3, while they struggled through the crowds following the signs to the *Mona Lisa* to tell Mr. Jones and Mr. Coatsworth.

# The Mona Lisa

"Mr. Jones!" Morgan shouted, catching up with him and Mr. Coatsworth as they stood behind Miss Parker, who had stopped abruptly in a doorway.

"Sssh!" said Mr. Jones, nodding towards Miss Parker, who was gazing reverently across the room.

"There it is!" Miss Parker breathed, staring at a glass box on the wall. "The *Mona Lisa*!"

"Mr. Jones?" Morgan repeated, tugging at his sleeve.

"Priceless," Miss Parker continued. "Leonardo's masterpiece!"

She winced and staggered, as the rest of Class 3 charged into the room, shouting for Mr. Jones.

"Oh!" she cried. "My leg!"

The children, who were about to tell Mr. Jones and Mr. Coatsworth what Matthew had told them, fell silent and stared at Miss Parker as she collapsed on the floor, clutching her bandaged leg.

"Oh!" she shrieked again. Mr. Coatsworth, bending over her in concern, attempted to help her up. The crowd of people who had been clustered round the *Mona Lisa* came rushing towards them to see what was going on. The guards, wondering what all the commotion was about, came rushing over too.

"Oh!" screamed Jessica, as Miss Parker's shrieks were drowned by the crash of breaking glass. "Look!"

Everyone gazed in horror at the shattered glass case as a loud wailing noise filled the room.

Standing next to the case was a man;
in one hand he clutched a gun, and
in the other, the *Mona Lisa*.

# 14
# Held Hostage

The guards looked at each other in alarm as the man tucked the painting under his arm, grabbed Jessica, and holding her like a shield, backed out of the door.

Mr. Jones, Mr. Coatsworth and the rest of Class 3 stood rooted to the spot, gazing in shocked silence as the man ran with the struggling Jessica through the next room towards the stairs.

"Quick! After them!" Avril screamed, and still grasping her bunch of balloons, ran after them.

"Wait!" said Mr. Jones as the rest of the children charged after Avril. "He's got a gun!"

"Oh dear," he murmured. The children, not hearing him, had vanished down the stairs.

"Mr. Coatsworth," he shouted, as Mr. Coatsworth prepared to give chase too. "Get Miss Parker into a taxi and back to the hotel. I've got to try and stop those children." Then, ignoring Mr. Coatsworth's protests, he ran after them, followed by the guards and the rest of the people in the room.

There were police cars all over the forecourt and gendarmes everywhere as Mr. Jones raced down the steps of the Louvre. He could see the gunman in the distance, still holding Jessica, as he ran across the forecourt towards the main road. The gendarmes, who had been warned that the man was armed and had taken a hostage, were shouting

through megaphones as they tried unsuccessfully to stop the rest of Class 3 from following the two figures.

The gunman had reached the wall surrounding the Louvre. He struggled over it, then, dodging in and out of the traffic, ran across the road to the Métro.

The children vaulted the wall, then stopped, waiting for the road to clear. Mr. Jones caught up with them as they dashed across the road.

"There he is!" screamed Avril, pointing to the Métro entrance. "After him!" The gunman, hearing her, turned and, throwing Jessica down, levelled his gun at the children as he backed down the tunnel steps. Class 3, ignoring Mr. Jones's shouts, had started down the steps too. They froze at the explosion that followed.

"Oh!" shrieked Avril, clutching her chest as she slid to the ground. "He got me!"

Mr. Jones, who was bending over the motionless body of Jessica, jumped up in alarm as Avril, who had been gingerly feeling her body for the bullet hole, stood up and gazed at her wet, crimson fingers in horror. "Blimey!" she whispered. "Blood!"

Jessica sat up. She looked at the sticky mess oozing from Avril's pocket. "Huh!" she sniffed disdainfully. "That's not blood. It's tomato ketchup!"

Everyone gazed at the balloons, and the shrivelled piece of blue rubber dangling from the bunch. "He didn't shoot you, either," Avril added. "It was just one of your balloons popping."

Then, eyeing Mr. Jones, she gave a little moan, and fell back again. "He nearly got me though," she gasped.

"Come on," shouted Morgan, hearing the distant rumble of a train, "he's getting away!"

"Oh no you don't!" thundered Mr. Jones, stopping the children in their tracks, as Avril removed the broken ketchup bottle from her pocket and ran to join them. He nodded to the gendarmes who were swarming towards them. "They can handle it now."

"Oh!" shrieked Jessica. "It was *awful*! Simply *awful* . . ." she repeated, her voice trailing off as she gazed after them dashing past her. "Don't they want to question me?" she added indignantly as they charged down to the Métro. The rest of the children, clustered round the entrance, gazed longingly after them. An agitated figure came running towards them.

"Thank goodness you're all right," said Mr. Coatsworth breathlessly. "I got Miss Parker into a taxi and came as quickly as I could, but those French policemen kept trying to stop me." He looked at Jessica. "How are you feeling?" he asked in concern.

"Dreadful," Jessica whispered. "It was simply *dreadful*!" She took a deep breath, her eyes shining. "It was like this . . ."

"Excuse me!" Someone tapped Mr. Jones on the shoulder. "Is that nice teacher with you?"

It was the bearded man, whom they'd met at the Eiffel Tower. He was still clutching the wilting flowers in his hand. "She'd left the hotel when I arrived," he continued, panting. "And the manager said he thought she was joining you at the Louvre. What's going on?" he added in alarm, seeing the grim-faced gendarmes emerging empty-handed from the tunnel.

"Someone has stolen the *Mona Lisa*," said Mr. Jones.

The man gasped, and the flowers fell from his hand.

"Miss Parker collapsed in the Louvre," Mr. Jones added. "She's gone back to the hotel."

"Oh!" cried Jessica, who had been so busy describing her lucky escape to Mr. Coatsworth that she'd only just noticed the bearded man. "The kidnapper! Morgan! Matthew! Sacha!" she shouted. "It's the kidnapper! The one whose photograph was in the newspaper!"

"What newspaper?" asked Mr. Jones in surprise

as the man, who had turned very pale, hastily turned his collar up, darted to the road and jumped into a taxi.

"Where?" cried Morgan, as he and the rest of the children ran out of the tunnel entrance.

"There!" said Jessica, pointing at the taxi vanishing into the distance.

"Crikey!" whispered Sacha, as a big black Citroën pulled away from the kerb.

"Crumbs!" exclaimed Matthew.

"16 90 75!" Morgan yelled.

# 15
# Under Arrest!

Crowds of curious bystanders joined the hordes of gendarmes and reporters who were milling around Class 3 asking questions and taking photographs. Morgan, Matthew and Sacha tried to explain to Mr. Jones and Mr. Coatsworth that it was the same car that they'd seen in New End, on the boat and following the doctor's car to Paris.

"Are you absolutely sure?" Mr. Jones asked. "It seems an incredible coincidence."

Morgan pulled from his pocket the piece of paper with the car's number on it and handed it to him. "I wrote it down in Dover," he said.

"Good Heavens!" Mr. Jones exclaimed, looking at the paper. "The number is identical. How amazing!"

"It looked to me," said Mr. Coatsworth,

puzzled, "as though he was following the other bearded chap."

"Who had his photo in the newspaper," Avril added.

"Where did you see this photograph?" Mr. Jones asked.

"In the newspaper the girl at the ticket office was reading," Morgan replied. "Sacha tried to read what it said about him, but he didn't have much time."

"I could understand only a few words," said Sacha. "Something about paintings."

"Perhaps we could go back and ask to see it again," Akbar suggested.

Mr. Coatsworth shook his head. "We can't," he said. "They've closed the Louvre to look for clues."

"Well!" said Mr. Jones. "We can see if there's a copy at the hotel when we get back."

"I doubt it," said Morgan. "It was yesterday's paper. That's why I noticed it. I thought it was strange that she should be reading an old newspaper."

Mr. Jones sighed. "There's a lot of strange things going on," he agreed.

Morgan looked at Sacha and Matthew. "I think we'd better tell you about the waiter," he added, as Matthew and Sacha nodded. "We didn't tell you before in case you didn't believe us."

Mr. Jones sighed again. "Morgan," he said, "if someone had told me that Hampstead Primary School's Class 3 would witness the theft of the *Mona Lisa*, I'd never have believed them. Right now I'll believe anything, but you'd better tell me on the way back to the hotel," he added, waving to Jessica, who reluctantly left the reporters and came over to join them. "We'd better get away from here while we can," he finished, as the excited crowd, realizing that the *Mona Lisa* had been stolen, shouted the news to passersby. The chief detective in charge of the robbery asked them a few more questions. Then, telling them not to leave Paris for the next six hours in case he needed to question them again, he said they could go.

They fought their way through the crowds to the bus stop—the gendarmes had sealed off the Métro entrance. Pursued by an excited mob who had discovered that they were witnesses to the crime, they escaped on a bus that was going to the Madeleine.

Mr. Jones sighed with relief as the bus pulled away from the disappointed crowd. Sitting next to Mr. Coatsworth, he listened carefully as Morgan told them about the button, the doctor's room number and the waiter's telephone conversations.

"So," said Mr. Jones, holding up a finger when Morgan had finished, "one, a black Citroën follows us to the ferry."

"No," Matthew interrupted. "It followed the

taxi to the ferry. The taxi was following us."

"All right," said Mr. Jones. "One," he repeated, "a taxi follows us to the ferry." He held up another finger. "Two," he said, "a black Citroën follows the taxi to the ferry. Three, the black Citroën follows the doctor's car to Paris."

"So the doctor," said Sacha, "must have been in the taxi."

"And picked up his own car at Calais," Morgan added.

"Four," said Mr. Jones, "the man in the black Citroën disappears. And the waiter tries to break into the doctor's room."

"But comes into mine instead," said Jessica proudly.

"Five," continued Mr. Jones, "the waiter goes to Calais and the other bearded chap from the ferry turns up."

"Followed by a balloon seller," Avril said, looking at her balloons.

"And finally," Mr. Jones said, "the bearded man turns up again and is followed, we think, by the black Citroën, which has suddenly reappeared. What do you make of it?" he asked, looking at Mr.

125

Coatsworth, who was gazing blankly at him.

"I don't know," admitted Mr. Coatsworth, standing up as the bus approached their stop. "It beats me."

Mr. Jones, Mr. Coatsworth and the children walked slowly back to the hotel, so busy discussing the strange things that were happening on their trip that they'd forgotten all about Miss Parker.

It wasn't until they'd reached the hotel entrance that Akbar mentioned her. Mr. Coatsworth remembered that Miss Parker had been reading a French newspaper on the journey to Paris, and, wondering if it was the one with the bearded man's photograph in, went to the car park to see if it was still in the bus.

"I do hope her leg is better," said Mr. Jones, pushing the hotel door open. "She seemed in a lot of pain. We'll go up to her room and see how she is," he added, as the children streamed into the hotel.

"Oh!" said Jessica, looking round the deserted lobby in disappointment. "There's no one here!"

"There must be," said Morgan, frowning. "I

can hear someone whispering."

"Here he is," said Mr. Jones, as the manager peered furtively from behind the restaurant door.

"I was taken hostage by a gunman," Jessica shouted at him. "He took me and the *Mona Lisa*!"

"Ah!" said the manager, mopping his brow with a handkerchief. "I heard about that dreadful business. Terrible! Terrible!" he repeated, glancing behind him as he slipped through the gap in the doorway.

Morgan, who had heard a movement behind the door, glanced at Sacha and Matthew, then at the door again, which was moving slightly.

"Is Miss Parker in her room?" Mr. Jones asked. The manager, his eyes travelling from the hotel entrance to the restaurant door, spotted a rolled package on the desk.

"She went to her room," he said, glancing at the name on the package. "She asked not to be disturbed." He handed the package to Mr. Jones. "For you," he added, looking at the entrance again.

"Who on earth could have sent it?" asked Mr. Jones, examining the parcel.

127

"I did not see who brought it," said the manager. "Whoever did just left it on the desk."

Mr. Jones unwrapped the parcel while the children, noticing the restaurant door opening, looked to see who was behind it.

"Good Heavens!" cried Mr. Jones, as the wrapping paper fell to the floor.

*"Mon Dieu!"* whispered the manager faintly.

The children, still staring at the door, didn't see what Mr. Jones was holding in his hand. They gasped as a bearded figure emerged, stopped, looked at Mr. Jones, then flung himself at him. Class 3 leaped at the man, caught him in mid-flight and pinned him to the floor.

The manager, in his excitement, was hopping from one foot to the other, shouting in French.

The front door swung open and Mr. Coatsworth burst in. "Hey!" he shouted. "That black Citroën's in the car park!"

He stopped in alarm when he saw the struggling figures on the floor.

"We know!" cried Jessica, tugging at the man's beard. "We've caught the bearded man who was in it!"

128

"No we ain't!" shouted Avril, staring at the moustache that was left on the man's face. "It's the waiter!"

"No, it's not!" yelled Morgan, as Akbar, hoping the moustache was false too, pulled it off. "It's the balloon seller!"

"Stop! Stop!" cried the manager, remembering his English. He ran from behind the desk. "He is not a waiter. He is not a balloon seller." He paused. "He is Detective Inspector Thoreau of the French Police!"

"And you, Monsieur," said the Inspector, looking at Mr. Jones as the children loosened their grip on him, "are under arrest!"

Class 3 gazed in silence at the painting their dazed teacher was still clutching in his hand.

# 16
# The Newspaper Article

Mr. Jones, who had been too shocked to move during the commotion, was still staring at the painting. He opened his mouth, but as no sound came out, he shut it again.

Mr. Coatsworth could hardly believe his eyes. "The *Mona Lisa*," he whispered, as the children, stunned, gazed blankly at the detective.

The manager, eyeing Mr. Jones apprehensively, helped the Inspector to his feet.

"So!" murmured the detective, carefully detaching the painting from Mr. Jones's paralysed fingers. "I now realize why Harry the Forger stuck like glue to the school bus on the way to the ferry." He shook his head. "I was on the wrong side of the track with the doctor." He sighed. "I could not believe my eyes when I saw Harry contacting you; who would suspect a teacher visiting Paris with a class of schoolchildren?" He shook his head again. "I suppose Harry wanted this to copy so he could flood the art market with fake *Mona Lisa*'s. Impossible!" he added passionately. "There will only ever be one *Mona Lisa*!

"And now," he continued, looking at Mr. Jones, who was still staring at the painting, "perhaps you will tell us where Harry is?"

Mr. Coatsworth and the children listened, open-mouthed, too astonished to interrupt.

"Never mind," said the detective, when Mr. Jones only blinked at him. "We'll pick him up. And the hired hood who stole the *Mona Lisa*!"

He spoke to the manager in French, who nodded and picked up the telephone.

"And now, Monsieur," he said, taking a pair of handcuffs from his pocket and snapping them on the unprotesting teacher's wrists. "Will you kindly come with me? And you, Monsieur," he added, nodding to Mr. Coatsworth, "I suggest you tell the other teacher to take these children back to England. But you will stay in Paris, please. I may need to question you later."

Morgan was the first to come out of the trance.

"Wait!" he cried, jumping up as the Inspector led Mr. Jones, who had a glazed look on his face, towards the door.

The rest of Class 3 jumped up too and, followed by Mr. Coatsworth, dashed after Morgan, who was running after the Inspector. Their way was barred by two grim-faced gendarmes. Mr. Coatsworth and the children watched helplessly, their faces pressed against the glass door, as a third gendarme drove the Citroën to the front of the hotel and the Inspector bundled Mr. Jones into it.

"What can we do?" Matthew asked forlornly.

"Nothing at the moment." Mr. Coatsworth sighed. "We'll just have to wait."

"I wonder why the *Mona Lisa* was left for Mr. Jones," said Akbar, bewildered.

"And who left it," muttered Avril.

"And why the Inspector just happened to be at the hotel when Mr. Jones opened the parcel," said Morgan.

"The Inspector mentioned a forger," said Mr. Coatsworth, frowning. "I wonder whom he meant?"

"The bearded man from the boat!" Sacha cried. "It said something about paintings under his photograph. I bet he's Harry the Forger! That's why the man from the Citroën, I mean the Inspector," he corrected himself, "started to follow him on the ferry when the doctor and Miss Parker took him to the bar! I wish we could get hold of a copy of that newspaper," he added.

"But we've got one!" said Mr. Coatsworth. "I found it on the bus. I clean forgot about it with all this carry-on." He pulled the paper out of his pocket.

"It was the one Miss Parker was reading," he added, handing it to Sacha. "It's even folded at the right page."

"So she must have seen the photograph," Morgan murmured, as Sacha studied the paper. "I wonder why she didn't mention it."

"*Contrefaçon*," Sacha cried, pointing at the word. "That means forgery!"

Morgan, who had a puzzled frown on his face, suddenly whistled. "The detective must have thought the forger was arranging the robbery with Mr. Jones when he was really asking where Miss Parker was. Don't you think it's odd," he added, "that he should want to deliver a bunch of flowers to Miss Parker in the middle of organizing a robbery—" His voice trailed off when he realized

135

that Mr. Coatsworth and the rest of Class 3 were so engrossed in the newspaper that they hadn't heard him and were following Sacha who was carrying it to the manager to ask him to translate it.

Morgan walked over to the manager too and stood behind the children crowded round him. The manager, looking at Mr. Coatsworth uncertainly, took the newspaper.

"What does it say?" Jessica demanded.

"It says," said the manager, as Morgan bent down to pick up from the floor the paper that had been wrapped round the *Mona Lisa*, "that this man, known as Harry the Forger, is wanted by the French police in connection with a series of art forgeries sold to galleries in France as original paintings."

"That's why the girl at the Louvre was so interested," Sacha interrupted. The manager glanced nervously at Mr. Coatsworth and seeing the puzzled expression on his face, decided he wasn't in league with Mr. Jones after all.

"Detective Inspector Thoreau was very, very angry about this photograph," he whispered confi-

136

dentially. "He did not want the press involved until he had caught him. That is why he went to London," he continued, "and followed him to the ferry. He hoped to catch him when he delivered the forgeries in France. How do you say?" He frowned. "*Ah, oui!* Red-handed!"

"Yes," muttered Sacha, glancing at Morgan, who was busy studying the wrapping paper. "The Inspector said it was the forger in the taxi."

"And not the doctor as we thought," said Matthew. "Then why was he so interested in the doctor?"

"Ah!" The manager beckoned the children to come closer. "It seems that the forger must have realized he was being followed and hid himself on the boat and returned to England."

"Yes, but where does the doctor fit in?" Matthew insisted.

"Well!" whispered the manager. "It also seems that the doctor was the last person to have contact with the forger. Inspector Thoreau suspected they might be working together and that the forger might have slipped to the doctor whatever fake

painting he was carrying. So he followed the doctor to my hotel and pretended to be a waiter. And that is why he entered your room," he added apologetically to Jessica, who smiled proudly. "He thought it was the doctor's room. However," the manager continued, "he had a telephone call from a colleague in England this morning saying, as he later told me, that Harry the Forger had got on the ferry. So he went to Calais and followed him back to Paris."

"Why didn't he arrest him in Calais?" Akbar asked.

"I can only guess," said the manager, "that, as I said before, he was waiting to catch him red-handed. However, he followed the forger to the Eiffel Tower . . ."

"Disguised as a balloon seller," said Avril, looking at her balloons, which were slowly deflating.

The manager sighed again. "He was deeply shocked when he saw the forger had arranged to meet your Mr. Jones." He shook his head sadly. "Such a nice man. Such a gourmet. Who would have thought . . . ? Ah, well," he shrugged his shoulders.

"But that ain't true!" Avril cried indignantly. "Nobody arranged anything. That forger only asked him where Miss Parker was."

The manager frowned and stroked his chin. "Ah," he murmured. "That is so. He came and asked me which room she was in, but she had already left in a taxi for to go to the Louvre. He then departed very rapidly and the Inspector came in, showed me his photograph and asked if I'd seen

139

him. The rest you know. Inspector Thoreau followed him to the Louvre, saw him talking with your teacher by the Métro entrance and followed him. Unfortunately the traffic was very heavy and by the time the Inspector arrived back here the forger must have met the gunman somewhere, retrieved the *Mona Lisa* and sneaked it back here for your Mr. Jones to collect."

Morgan, who had been examining the wrapping paper while listening to the manager, suddenly sniffed his fingers.

"No, he didn't," he shouted, beckoning to Mr. Coatsworth and the rest of Class 3.

And while the perplexed manager gazed after them, Mr. Coatsworth and the other children charged up the stairs after Morgan, who was still clutching the wrapping paper in his hands.

# 17
# Suspicions

"Where are we going?" Mr. Coatsworth shouted as he and the children tried to catch up with Morgan.

"To see Miss Parker," said Morgan grimly, stopping on the first floor landing. "What room number is she?"

"Room 12," Mr. Coatsworth replied. "But what's all the hurry?"

"I want to ask her some questions," said Morgan, bounding up the second flight of stairs.

The rest of the children were shouting questions at Morgan as they raced after him to Room 12, but fell silent when he turned, put his finger to his lips and knocked.

The door slowly opened and Miss Parker stood there. She glanced briefly at the wrapping paper in Morgan's hand and then her gaze swept over the rest of the children who, not knowing why they were there, shifted uncomfortably.

"What is it you want?" she asked, turning to Morgan.

"Mr. Jones has been arrested," said Jessica as Morgan, looking at Miss Parker's face, hesitated.

"Really?" said Miss Parker. "But that is dreadful!"

"And we'd like to ask you a few questions," Morgan said nervously.

"I think," said Miss Parker, her eyes hardening as she opened the door wider, "that you had better come in! Now!" she said, sitting down as the children streamed into the room, looking a little confused, followed by Mr. Coatsworth who was looking very confused. "What is it you would like to know?"

"Er, how your leg is?" suggested Mr. Coatsworth, nudging Morgan.

"No," said Morgan bluntly. "Why was the forger following you?"

"Morgan!" said Mr. Coatsworth, shocked.

"I do not have a faint idea of what you are talking about," said Miss Parker quietly.

"You were very interested in the article about

him," Morgan persisted, ignoring Mr. Coatsworth's frantic gestures to stop. "You must have recognized the photo of the man from the boat."

"I read many articles," Miss Parker said calmly. "I find it impossible them all to remember."

"And your leg," Morgan went on. "This morning you said that you'd slept well, then you said it had been bothering you all night."

"I did not mention my leg hurting," Miss Parker replied, "because I did not want to miss the boat ride on the wonderful Seine. However," she

added, smiling at Mr. Coatsworth, who was looking terribly embarrassed, "I knew it would be difficult for me walking around the Louvre with it paining—that is quite different to sitting on a boat. So I rested it so I did not have to miss the *Mona Lisa*." She sighed. "And to think I never had the chance to look at it properly."

"I think you've had plenty of chances to look at it properly," Morgan said. He handed the wrapping paper to Mr. Coatsworth. "Smell this!"

Mr. Coatsworth took the paper and sniffed the faint familiar smell of French perfume.

"It's your perfume," he whispered, gazing at Miss Parker, who gazed back at him unconcerned.

"So," she said, taking the paper from his hand. "A piece of paper smells of the same perfume as I do. Well? Many people in France use this perfume." She dropped the paper to the floor. "Are you trying to accuse me of something?" she murmured, lowering her eyelashes.

"Oh, no! Heaven forbid!" cried Mr. Coatsworth, frowning at Morgan. "Come on, children, I think we should leave and let Miss Parker rest . . ."

"Because," Miss Parker interrupted, "I have

been in my room since I returned from the Louvre, I have nowhere been near the reception desk . . ." her voice trailed off and she looked sharply at Morgan.

"How did you know," Morgan asked quietly, "that it came from the reception desk?"

Miss Parker leaped out of her chair, her face white with fury. "So!" she hissed. "A smart brat! Too smart, though! Don't move!" she shrieked as Matthew and Sacha made for the door. "Stay where you are! If you do not," she added menacingly, "you will regret it."

She picked up the telephone as Matthew and Sacha moved away from the door as though hypnotized.

Everyone watched in horrified silence, too stunned to move, as she dialled a number, spoke quickly in French, then handed the receiver to Morgan.

"Now let us see", she said smiling again, "what you most value. The *Mona Lisa* or—" She took the receiver from Morgan's hand and replaced it.

"Miss Barker!" Morgan whispered faintly.

"It can't be," cried Mr. Coatsworth.

"Perhaps this will convince you," said Miss Parker, feeling in her handbag and holding up Miss Barker's passport. "My trump card!" she added, casually dropping the passport back into her handbag as the children gasped.

"And now, Mr. Coatsworth, you are going to take us all for a little ride. And if you are good little girls and boys," she continued, "Miss Barker will to no harm come. But if you are bad little girls and boys—" she sighed and shook her head—"poor Miss Barker," she murmured, walking towards the door. "Come along, now," she added, glancing over her shoulder at the dejected children.

The manager was still standing at the reception

desk as they trailed gloomily down the stairs behind Mr. Coatsworth and Miss Parker. Miss Parker stopped and spoke to the manager in French, who nodded sympathetically as he listened to her.

"I was telling him—" Miss Parker turned to Mr. Coatsworth as she pushed open the front door— "about the little trip we had arranged to try and cheer these poor children up. He is not us expecting back for supper."

"Where are you taking us?" Mr. Coatsworth demanded. "If any of these kids gets harmed . . ."

"Not a rabbit on their heads will be harmed," Miss Parker interrupted, "as long as they do as they are told. We are going to visit Miss Barker. I think it would be very nice if you did stay the night, all of you, to keep her company."

"You'll never get away with it," Mr. Coatsworth muttered grimly. "Once the police realize their mistake and release Mr. Jones . . ."

Miss Parker's harsh laugh interrupted him. "By that time," she added softly, "I will be many, many miles away. And now," she continued, as they stepped out onto the pavement, "for our little bus ride.

"Remember," Miss Parker hissed, "we are expected in one hour. One hour," she repeated, glancing round at the children who were trying to decide whether to make a run for it or not. "All of us. If we are not there in that time, it will be very, very unpleasant for your Miss Barker."

The children, not liking the tone of her voice, gave up any thoughts of escape and reluctantly followed her and Mr. Coatsworth to the car park.

"Do you think she's bluffing?" Matthew whispered to Morgan. "Do you think she really has got Miss Barker prisoner?"

Morgan nodded. "Yes," he whispered back. "It was Miss Barker's voice all right. And don't forget Polly and Peter said they'd seen her in Paris. Anyway," he added, "Miss Parker has her passport."

"What if it was just a recording of Miss Barker's voice?" Matthew asked. "Polly and Peter could have been mistaken. And the passport could have been a forged one."

"What I can't understand," said Sacha, as

Morgan gasped, "is why she left the *Mona Lisa* for Mr. Jones."

"Of course!" Morgan cried. "That's it!" He lowered his voice as Miss Parker turned and looked at him. "She didn't leave him the *Mona Lisa*!" he hissed excitedly.

"But you just accused her of it!" Sacha protested as Miss Parker started pushing the children in front of them onto the bus.

"Don't you see?" said Morgan slowly. "She left Mr. Jones *a Mona Lisa*. Not *the Mona Lisa*!"

"Crikey!" said Matthew, shaking his head in disbelief. "You mean she left Mr. Jones a fake?"

Morgan nodded. "To put the police off the scent, I suppose. Until the real *Mona Lisa* was safely out of the way."

Matthew and Sacha looked at each other. "Harry the Forger," whispered Sacha. "He did the fake! That's why he was following her around!"

"I'd like to know where the real one is," Morgan muttered, as Miss Parker, having grabbed Avril's balloons, released them into the air and pushed her

onto the bus, then turned and motioned to the three boys to get on.

"Now," said Miss Parker, when everyone was on the bus. "Château St. Germain! I will direct you," she added.

Mr. Coatsworth sighed wearily and started the engine.

"Château St. Germain," Morgan whispered. "I wonder if that's the same *château* the doctor visited?"

Matthew sighed too, as the bus started forward, and the silent children gazed miserably out of the windows. "I expect we'll find out soon," he murmured.

# 18
# The Journey

The children were much too miserable to enjoy the ride. The huge, stately buildings that they passed as they drove through the centre of Paris didn't impress them at all. The pretty cobbled streets and the elegant houses with their grey slate roofs dotted with attic windows didn't excite them, either, and in the fading afternoon light, the wide avenues lined with chestnut trees and pavement cafés seemed positively ominous to the children.

Soon they were on a main road passing tall concrete blocks of apartments. The blocks gradually gave way to scrubby-looking fields and then, quite suddenly, the bus turned and they were in a dark country lane. Miss Parker turned to face the children.

"We are close now," she said, glancing at her watch. "Miss Barker will be most pleased that you will not be late. Left here," she added to Mr. Coatsworth.

She faced the children again. "Remember," she said softly, as the children murmured amongst themselves, "you must act like good little English children who have invited been to stay the night at this beautiful *château*. Miss Barker will be sorry extremely if you misbehave." She felt in her handbag and held up a tiny gun. "And you might be, also," she threatened as the children stared at it in dismay.

Mr. Coatsworth, who had opened his mouth to protest, closed it again when he saw the gun.

Shrugging helplessly, he swung the bus into the turning. A gateway was in front of them and through the closed iron gates they could just see the shape of a big house at the end of the drive.

"You will wait here," said Miss Parker as the bus stopped.

"What shall we do?" Morgan asked desperately. Miss Parker had dropped the gun back into her handbag, climbed out of the bus and rung the bell of the lodge house next to the gates.

"There's not much we can do," said Mr. Coatsworth grimly, interrupting the children who had

all started talking at once.

"Couldn't we make a run for it," Sacha whispered, "and try and contact the police?"

Mr. Coatsworth shook his head. "You heard what she said about Miss Barker. We can't risk it."

"Maybe she wouldn't miss one of us," Akbar said. "I could slip out now while she's not looking."

Mr. Coatsworth shook his head again, watching Miss Parker who seemed to be arguing with an old man who had emerged from the lodge house. "It's too dangerous," he said. "She's quite likely to use that gun!"

The iron gates creaked open, and Miss Parker nodded to Mr. Coatsworth, who drove the bus forward along the gravelled drive.

"Look!" Morgan whispered, grabbing Matthew's pen from his hand and nodding to the big American car parked in front of the *château*.

He quickly wrote the registration number on the back of his hand.

"I thought we'd bump into him again," he murmured, as the doctor appeared in the doorway.

Miss Parker pulled the gun from her bag and jerked it towards the bus door. "Everybody out," she said. "And no tricks!"

She led them into an enormous room, where dust sheets covered the bulky furniture. They followed her through several smaller rooms, then through a passageway and down a flight of stone steps to a damp cellar. The doctor trailed behind them, holding a gun. She stopped by a door where two men were playing cards.

"Oh!" cried Jessica, as one of the men looked up. "It's him! The man who stole the *Mona Lisa*! And me," she added, clutching Mr. Coatsworth's arm tightly.

The man grinned and pulled a key from his pocket.

"And now," said Miss Parker, unlocking the door and indicating with the gun for Mr. Coatsworth and the children to enter the room, "to meet your precious Miss Barker!"

And before their eyes could get accustomed to the dim light, they were pushed roughly into the cellar.

# 19
## Prisoners!

The only light in the cellar came from a single naked bulb. Through the gloom they saw their headmistress. She jumped to her feet when she saw them.

"Oh! My darlings!" she exclaimed, throwing her arms around as many of the children as they would encompass.

"Jessica! Luke! Avril! Akbar!" she cried, lifting them up and tossing them in the air before catching them and pressing them to her ample bosom.

"She didn't harm you, my little lambs, did she?" she asked anxiously, still clutching Akbar and glaring at Miss Parker who stood in the doorway with a thin smile on her lips.

Suddenly Miss Barker screamed and dropped Akbar. "If that creature comes anywhere near me," she shrieked, stabbing a finger at the doctor, who was peeping behind the door, "I'll flatten him!"

She grabbed Jessica and Avril, who were nearest to her, as Akbar, still trying to get his breath back, crawled over to join the rest of the children, who had backed out of reach of Miss Barker's outstretched arms and were panting in a corner.

"Never put your trust in a man," she said, gazing earnestly into Avril and Jessica's eyes before hugging them again. "Promise me. Make them promise!" she implored Mr. Coatsworth.

Jessica and Avril tried to reply, but couldn't, as Miss Barker had their faces pressed so firmly

against her stomach that they were beginning to suffocate. (In fact if Avril hadn't been a wrestling fan and thumped Miss Barker on the back the way she'd seen the Black Mombassa do it on TV, they probably would have.)

"We promise!" Avril and Jessica gasped, as Miss Barker loosened her grip of them. Mr. Coatsworth cleared his throat.

"Er, how did they get you here?" he asked timidly.

"Yes," drawled Miss Parker, "do tell them. It amuses me. But hurry." She looked at her watch. "I have a plane to catch. It was most thoughtful of you", she added, holding Miss Barker's passport up, "to have an American visa in your passport." She laughed harshly, twirling the gun in her other hand, as Miss Barker, swearing softly to herself, leaped at her.

"That woman!" Miss Barker exploded, shaking her fist at Miss Parker as Mr. Coatsworth pulled her back. "And, that, that snake in the grass!" she shrieked, looking over Miss Parker's shoulder, trying to spot the doctor, who had dodged behind the door again.

"Fooled me! Deceived me! Took me for a ride. Oooh!" she added, her arms flaying as she struggled to free herself from Mr. Coatsworth's restraining hold.

"If only I could get my hands on them, I'd tear them limb from limb, I'd, I'd . . ." her voice faltered. Unable to find a description of what she'd do and overcome with emotion, she burst into tears.

"It all happened," she sobbed, "when I went into that little bookshop off Charing Cross Road to buy a postcard of the *Mona Lisa*. They were there," she nodded at Miss Parker and the doctor, who was peeping over the French teacher's shoulder again. "The rats! And little Harry."

"Who?" asked Akbar, who had got his breath back.

"Me," said a voice from the darkness.

"Crikey!" whispered Morgan, as a figure emerged from the shadows behind Miss Barker. "Harry the Forger!"

"Look out, Miss!" yelled Avril, rushing towards Miss Barker. "He's behind you!"

"It's all right, Avril precious," sniffed Miss Barker, and before Avril had time to move backward, she was enveloped in Miss Barker's arms again.

"But he's a forger!" Avril's muffled voice protested. "He's in league with Miss Parker!"

The rest of Class 3 stared at Miss Barker in surprise, as she nodded.

"He does do very nice copies," she admitted, "but I wouldn't exactly call him a forger." She looked fondly at Harry, who blushed, and lowered his eyes. "But he's not in league with that woman," she continued, still gazing at Harry. "Not any more. Although when I first met him he did have an

162

occasional business deal with them," she added sternly, wagging a finger at Harry, who shook his head repentantly.

"Anyway, as I was saying, I went into the bookshop to buy a postcard of the *Mona Lisa* to bring to school to show you. Then I saw Harry here with those two," she rolled her eyes in the direction of the door, "buying every book on Leonardo that they could lay their hands on. Harry then asked me if he could buy the postcard from me, as it was the only one left in the shop and he wanted to do a little copy of it. I, of course, said I couldn't part with it, as I was taking Class 3 to Paris to see the original *Mona Lisa*, and wanted my children to see what they would be looking at. Well, Harry left it at that, but those two skunks over there suddenly became very interested in me and asked me if I travelled a lot and had I been to America."

Miss Barker sighed and clutched Avril even tighter.

"Of course I told them that I'd just had my American visa stamped in my passport as I was planning a holiday in Las Vegas in the summer."

"But how did she get your passport?" Morgan asked, as Miss Barker stopped for breath.

"And how did you get to France without it?" Matthew added.

Miss Barker sighed again.

"I'm afraid, darling hearts, that I have a confession to make. That overripe camembert over there," she jerked her head towards the doctor again, "invited me out for dinner, asked me what my interests were, and when I told him how passionately I loved musicals and how I was hoping to get to see the new Jess Conrad musical in Paris, he told me the show was fully booked up but he had two tickets for the opening night." She shook her head. "And like a fool I believed him."

She glanced down at Avril and, noticing her threshing feet, gently detached her from her bosom.

"But how did they get you here?" Matthew insisted.

"I bet they tied you up, and smuggled you into France in the boot of a car!" Jessica whispered.

"Oh Jessica!" Miss Barker wailed, reaching out to her. "It was first class Air France and champagne all the way! It's all my fault," she added, as Jessica did a neat sidestep, pushing Matthew forward instead. "Everything is my fault," she cried, grabbing Matthew as he stumbled.

"Poor Mr. Jones is held by the police because of me. You're held prisoner because of me. I'm a very foolish woman." She blew her nose loudly, pinning Matthew down with her free arm.

"Doctor Jekyll over there, having buttered me up, suggested I go to the concert in Paris with him as his elderly mother, whom he'd planned to take, had twisted her ankle and wouldn't be able to make it. Of course I told him that I couldn't possibly as it would mean taking most of the day off on Thursday to get to Paris and most of Friday morning to get back, as the concert finished too late to catch a flight back on Thursday, and who would take my little angels for French? Then that viper over there, who had joined us for coffee, said she was a trained teacher and would be happy to take over my class for two days until I got back.

"Oh!" she cried, bursting into tears again. "What a fool I was! I fell for their little trick and as I was owed two days' holiday, I rang the school

165

secretary to tell her I'd arranged for a replacement teacher for two days but would be back at school in time for the school trip. Which, of course, I expected to be. Then that vixen arrived at the school, told the secretary that I had telephoned her to ask if she would take my place on the school trip to Paris as I'd been taken to hospital with suspected appendicitis and expected to be in quite a few days. And, of course, she told her that I'd forgotten to mention which hospital it was. So, like a lamb to the slaughter, I was brought to this place."

"There! There!" said Mr. Coatsworth soothingly as she burst into fresh floods of tears.

"He was so charming on the journey." She sobbed. "I didn't suspect a thing when he asked me if I'd like to pop in and see his aged mother at her *château* before going to the theatre. It wasn't until he got me here, locked me up and took my passport that I realized I'd been tricked. And all he wanted was me out of the way so that creature could take my place on the school trip. It was the perfect situation for them. No one would suspect a teacher in charge of a class of schoolchildren of stealing the *Mona Lisa*!"

"They suspected Mr. Jones," Morgan murmured.

"They planted the copy that Harry did on him," Miss Barker sobbed. "They realized that if the police thought they'd got the *Mona Lisa* back, they'd call off the manhunt, which would give them time to get out of the country with the real one. Harry told me. You see poor Harry was double-crossed too."

Harry nodded gloomily.

"All Harry did was to sell paintings to them. I'm sure he wasn't aware that they were selling them to galleries as the genuine thing," she added, glancing at Harry, who shook his head vigorously.

"After all, he can't help it if Leonardo and Rembrandt paint in the same style as he does."

Miss Parker laughed sarcastically, but Miss Barker ignored her.

"Of course when she made off with his beautiful

167

likeness of the *Mona Lisa* without paying him for it, he was very upset. And when he heard that woman say she would replace me at school and discovered that she intended to come to Paris on the school trip, he put two and two together and followed the school bus to the ferry."

"But she wasn't on the school bus," said Sacha.

Miss Barker shook her head. "No. She had to meet that rat of a doctor to get my passport from him first."

"But why?" asked Akbar.

"Because she's a crook!" cried Miss Barker, glaring at Miss Parker.

"She didn't dare travel on her own passport in case the French police were on to her. That's why she called herself Miss Parker, so anyone seeing the name Barker on the passport and hearing her addressed as Miss Parker would assume it was the same name! That's why she dyed her hair, to fool the passport people! Anyway," she continued, "Harry, assuming they would be on the ferry, boarded it too. Of course he recognized her and went to ask her for his painting back!"

"That's why he was creeping up to them," said Jessica. "We thought he was trying to kidnap her!"

"Of course, when they saw him," Miss Barker went on, "they lured him to a deserted spot on the boat. Then they tied him up, gagged him and dumped him into a lifeboat. Poor Harry didn't free himself until the ferry had returned to Dover. But, still determined to find them, he took the next ferry to Calais, which wasn't until the next morning, went to Paris and quite rightly guessed that the first place a group of English children would want to visit would be the Eiffel Tower. Where, as you know, he spotted you."

Miss Barker stopped for breath again. "He didn't want to alarm you by telling you that your new French teacher was a crook, so he pretended he wanted to deliver some flowers to her. But when he did eventually get to see her, old ratface here," she indicated the doctor, who ducked behind Miss Parker, "was in the hotel room with her. No doubt looking for a suitable hiding place for the real *Mona Lisa*. Of course poor Harry didn't have a chance and ratface brought him here with a gun in his back! Then ratface tricked me into talking to you on the telephone," she finished, glancing at Morgan, before looking beseechingly at the rest of the children.

"A very touching story," Miss Parker interrupted. "But I am afraid I will have to shut you all up for a little while. You have talked enough." She turned and spoke to the two men guarding the door.

"I do not want that old fool of a lodgekeeper disturbed by any shouting," she added, as the two men entered the cellar carrying rope and bandages. Class 3 watched in dismay as the men bound and gagged Harry the Forger.

"I would not resist if I were you," Miss Parker warned Mr. Coatsworth, who was ready to spring at the men as they advanced towards the children. "Someone might get hurt!"

"Better do as she says, kids," he sighed, realizing it was useless to struggle.

It didn't take the men long to finish their work, even though the children, ignoring Mr. Coatsworth's advice, kicked and punched their captors while they were being bound and gagged.

"Good!" said Miss Parker in satisfaction, looking at the row of trussed-up bodies. She turned to the doctor and smiled.

"And now," she added softly, "for the airport."

# 20
# The Rescue

The children gazed silently at one another. They could hear the sound of the doctor's car fading away in the distance.

Some of the children tried to stand up, but with their wrists bound behind their backs it was difficult to balance, and the fact that their ankles were tied together didn't help either.

Then Matthew and Sacha started shuffling backward on their bottoms until they reached a wall. They pushed their backs against it and, edging themselves up, managed to stand. Then they hopped over to the door and shoved their bodies against it in desperation even though they knew it was useless, as they'd heard the click of the key in the lock when the crooks departed.

The rest of the children, having watched Matthew and Sacha, managed to get on their feet too, and started bobbing round the cellar looking for another way out. But there wasn't one.

Then Morgan, noticing a dark shape at the opposite end of the cellar, struggled over to it. It was a wine rack, and as he studied the bottles that were stacked in neat rows, he saw that the wine was champagne.

Then he remembered Christmas day when his dad had opened a bottle of champagne and how annoyed his mother had been when his dad shook the bottle and the cork shot out, knocking the fairy off the top of the Christmas tree. Jack and Charles from next door had come rushing in thinking there'd been a gas explosion.

Morgan twisted himself around so that his back was against the rack. Then feeling the neck of a bottle, he edged it forward so that while the bottle was resting in the rack, his fingers could work at the wire that released the cork. He managed to untwist the wire and dropped it to the floor. He pushed at the cork with his thumbs, the way he'd seen his dad do, until he felt the cork loosen. Quickly he pulled the bottle out of the rack and shook it vigorously.

Miss Barker, who had only just made it to her feet, screamed and slid slowly down the wall at the sudden explosion.

Mr. Coatsworth and the rest of the children saw Morgan jerking his head towards the wine rack.

Several of the children in their rush to get to the champagne fell over Harry (who was lying like a sack of potatoes in the middle of the cellar) and had to back up against the wall again before they could stand up and hop to the others, who were already eagerly working at the bottles.

The noise was so tremendous that Class 3 didn't even hear the key turn in the lock. The bewildered

face of the old lodgekeeper peered in at them. He gasped when he saw Miss Barker who, deciding it was the safest place to be, was still lying on the floor.

He hurried over to her and quickly untied the bandage round her mouth.

"Help! Police!" shrieked Miss Barker, as the man freed her wrists and ankles. Then, realizing the man couldn't understand her, repeated it in French. Miss Barker freed Mr. Coatsworth as the

175

man rushed to the door to telephone the police.

"Tell him to tell the police that they're heading for the airport," Mr. Coatsworth gasped, working at Sacha's gag.

"Tell him to give them a description of the car!" Sacha cried, pulling the bandage off Morgan's mouth.

"Tell him to tell them the registration number is MAL 1!" Morgan shouted, glancing down at his hand.

"And tell him not to forget to tell Detective Inspector Thoreau that Mr. Jones didn't steal the *Mona Lisa!*" yelled Jessica, when Miss Barker had removed her bandage too. "And that those crooks have it!"

The lodgekeeper ran out, repeating the instructions to himself so as not to forget them.

By the time the lodgekeeper returned, everyone was free. The children waited impatiently for Miss Barker to translate what the lodgekeeper was saying to her.

"Did he remember to tell them everything?" Avril demanded, when the man stopped for breath.

"Yes," said Miss Barker. "They've set up a road block and alerted the airport . . ."

"Let's hope they're not too late," Morgan muttered.

"Yes," agreed Mr. Coatsworth. "If they make it to America, it will be practically impossible to find them."

"Did he get the message to Inspector Thoreau?" Jessica asked.

Miss Barker nodded. "Yes. He's bringing Mr. Jones here. Apparently he wants to question the lodgekeeper."

"I think I'll just nip out for a breath of air," Harry murmured, as the lodgekeeper, who was getting more and more agitated, groaned and closed his eyes.

"What's wrong with him?" asked Akbar, as the man groaned again.

"The poor man seems convinced that the police will put him in jail," Miss Barker replied, blowing a kiss to Harry as he slipped out of the door. "He says they won't believe that he was only the lodge-keeper and had nothing to do with the crooks. He says," she continued, "that the *château* is normally

177

closed at this time of the year, but he'd received a letter from the owner, a multimillionaire, saying a friend of his would be using it, but not to bother about hiring staff as he would only be here for a few days."

The man spoke quickly to her again.

"Apparently," she added, "the owner only uses the *château* . . ." her voice trailed off, "when he's visiting Europe," she whispered, "looking for paintings to add to his collection!"

"That's it!" yelled Morgan.

"They're taking it to him!" screamed Avril.

"Of course!" breathed Mr. Coatsworth, as the children danced around the cellar with excitement. "And he lives in America! That's why she needed the visa!"

"I wonder how they planned to smuggle it through customs," Morgan murmured. The noise of screaming sirens drowned his words.

"Mr. Jones!" shrieked Jessica, running out of the cellar, followed by the rest of Class 3 and Mr. Coatsworth. The lodgekeeper trailed after them with Miss Barker, who had selected two bottles of vintage champagne to take with her.

178

"Golly!" cried Jessica, dazzled by car lights as she reached the doorway of the *château*. "Look at all those police cars! There's Mr. Jones!" she added as a car door opened.

"Isn't that the doctor and Miss Parker in the car behind?" Morgan asked, squinting at the cars.

"Why would they bring them back here?" asked Matthew.

"Let's go and find out," said Sacha, as more car doors opened and gendarmes spilled out.

"What's happening?" shouted Avril, as the children ran to Mr. Jones and Inspector Thoreau.

"They can't find the *Mona Lisa*," Mr. Jones replied. "They picked the crooks up on the way to the airport, but it wasn't on them. They think they must have hidden it in the *château*."

Inspector Thoreau sighed. "They will not talk," he said grimly, nodding towards the police car with the doctor and Miss Parker in it.

"They'll talk when I've finished with them," said Miss Barker, her blue eyes flashing. The police driver and the gendarme sitting between the two crooks were so amazed at the suddenness of Miss Barker's appearance that they only gasped when Miss Barker dragged Miss Parker out of the door. She probably would have made her talk too if she hadn't unfortunately slipped on the champagne bottles.

Miss Parker, sensing freedom, made for a darkened corner of the garden. But Class 3 were too quick for her and dived at her legs.

Avril was clinging to the bandage wrapped around Miss Parker's leg, as Miss Parker shook her leg, desperately trying to free herself. "Blimey!" muttered Avril. "The bandage is coming off!"

"Crikey!" whispered Matthew, as Jessica and Akbar threw themselves at Miss Parker, and catching her off balance, knocked her to the ground.

"Look!" He pointed to the bandage slowly unravelling itself.

"The *Mona Lisa*!" screamed the rest of Class 3.

# 21
# Guests of Honour

"Well!" said Mr. Jones later, as the children, dressed in their best clothes, stood in the lobby of the hotel. "It's going to be a very late night for the kids." He smiled, looking at the children who were noisily discussing the events of the day.

"Mind you," he added. "I don't think they would have got much sleep tonight anyway. They're much too excited. Although I must say," he continued, "it's awfully nice of the Inspector to invite us all to the Moulin Rouge for dinner."

"And to insist that we were chauffeur-driven there," said Mr. Coatsworth, looking through the glass doors at the line of immaculate black Citroëns waiting to take them to their destination.

"The poor man was dreadfully upset about detaining you at the police station," said Miss Barker, patting Mr. Jones's arm. "Although he did

182

tell me that the Leonardo expert was on his way from Italy to examine the painting. I'm sure they would have released you immediately once they'd discovered it wasn't the original *Mona Lisa*!"

"Yes," agreed Mr. Coatsworth, "but if the lodgekeeper hadn't released us from the cellar, the crooks would have been safely in America by then. And if Morgan hadn't smelled the perfume on the wrapping paper, they'd have almost certainly got away with it."

"She was a very clever woman," said Mr. Jones. "Convincing us that she'd spilled boiling fat on her leg, when really the bandage was hiding the fake *Mona Lisa*."

"And then the real one," Mr. Coatsworth added.

"Well, at least the police have them under lock and key now," said Miss Barker with satisfaction. She sighed. "It's a pity little Harry slipped away without saying good-bye," she murmured wistfully.

"I think perhaps it's as well he did," said Mr. Jones, remembering the Inspector's interest in him.

"What about that multimillionaire bloke?" Mr. Coatsworth asked. "Do you think they'll get him?"

"Almost certainly," Mr. Jones replied. "I heard the Inspector say they were sending a detective to America to interview him."

Mr. Coatsworth shook his head again. "It's been a rum couple of days," he remarked. "We haven't seen much of Paris, but by gum there's not been a dull moment."

Mr. Jones looked at his watch. "It's nine o'clock," he said. "We'd better be going."

"Come on, darling hearts!" Miss Barker shouted as she hurried to the door where the rest of the children were admiring the row of sleek, elegant cars. "We don't want to be late," she added, admiring the row of sleek, elegant chauffeurs who were standing next to the cars.

One of the chauffeurs escorted Mr. Jones and Matthew, Sacha and Morgan to the first car and when they were seated, climbed into the driver's seat to lead the stately procession to Montmartre.

"I wonder what all that noise is?" Morgan murmured, as they approached Place Blanche.

The three boys craned forward to look out of the front window.

They blinked at the glaring spotlights that were set up in front of the Moulin Rouge, illuminating the crowds who were shouting and waving Tricolours and Union Jacks. There were French TV cameras everywhere. Photographers started fighting for the best positions as the crowd, spotting the first car, cheered wildly.

Berets were thrown high in the air as the crowd surged forward and the gendarmes had to link arms to make a pathway for the procession.

When the children stepped out and waved at the crowds, a delighted roar went up. Cameras clicked and whirred as the children were hurriedly escorted into the famous Moulin Rouge.

The applause was so thunderous as they entered that the orchestra, who had struck up with the tune "Mona Lisa", were completely drowned.

Detective Inspector Thoreau, who was waiting to greet them, beamed as all the other guests (some of the most famous people in Paris), climbed onto their chairs to get a glimpse of the children, shouting, "*Vivat!*" and "*Magnifique!*"

"Welcome, welcome!" cried Inspector Thoreau, warmly embracing his guests as they lined up to greet him. The waiters cheered as he led the children to their table. The cancan girls peeped through the velvet curtains on the stage and cheered too, and the other guests left their tables and darted forward to shake the children's hands.

The mayor asked Mr. Jones if they could possibly manage a private luncheon at the Palace of Versailles, and the keeper of the Louvre asked Mr. Coatsworth if they would all join him on his luxury boat for a trip up the Seine. The manager of L'Opéra pleaded with Miss Barker for them to

attend the first night of a new comic opera and then have supper with him at the Folies Bergère. When Miss Barker said it was a pity the Jess Conrad show was sold out, he said his brother-in-law was manager of that theatre and he would get them all seats for that show too.

In fact, by the time they actually reached their table, they had so many invitations they were having to turn them down.

Avril's eyes lit up when she noticed the bottle of tomato ketchup that the chef had thoughtfully provided. Miss Barker's eyes lit up when she noticed the silver ice buckets where enormous bottles of the world's most expensive champagne nestled. (There were also several silver ice buckets where the world's most expensive bottles of Coca-Cola nestled, too.)

The Inspector held his hand up for silence.

"I know", he said, speaking English for the children's benefit, "that toasts and messages should come at the backside of dinner, but," he continued, patting the huge pile of telegrams on the table, "there is one very special message I have to read on the frontside." He lifted the top tele-

188

gram off the pile. "I will read the others later," he added, "as I am sure that our young guests are as hungry as a horse." He smiled at the children again, who, noticing the trolleys of mouth-watering food that the waiters had started wheeling in, nodded vigorously.

"This message", he said solemnly, holding the piece of paper up for everyone to see, "is from the President himself!" He waited for the *oohs!* and *ahs!* to die down before lowering it again.

"It says," he continued, as the TV cameras closed in on the table and the photographers held their cameras up expectantly, "that the President of France regrets that he cannot be with you on this momentous occasion, but sends his sincere and grateful thanks to the staff members and children of Class 3, Hampstead Primary School, for the great personal courage they have shown in recovering the nation's most famous painting, the *Mona Lisa*. But—" he held his hand up for silence again at the renewed cheering—"he would be most honoured," he shouted above the noise, "if along with the huge reward, you would return to Paris as his guest to receive the nation's greatest award."

He paused. Everyone fell silent. *"La Légion d'Honeur!"* he screamed ecstatically.

The chandeliers shook at the frenzied cheering that followed. The reporters and cameramen were beside themselves with excitement, swarming round the table as the waiters piled food onto it, shouting questions and taking photographs of Class 3, who sat open-mouthed, too stunned to move.

"Excuse me," said a voice from under the table. The man from the BBC, who had been knocked to the floor in the stampede, held a microphone up to Morgan's face.

"Would you mind awfully telling the viewers back home how it all happened?"

"Well!" said Morgan in a dazed voice. "It all happened when we noticed a French car following us in Hampstead."

"With a bearded stranger in it," said Jessica.

"Only it wasn't really following us," Matthew added. "It was following the taxi."

"And he wasn't really a bearded stranger," said Avril. "He was Inspector Thoreau!"

"And the taxi wasn't really following us," interrupted Sacha. "It was following Miss Parker!"

"Only she wasn't really Miss Parker," said Akbar. "And she wasn't on the bus, either."

"But I suppose," said Mr. Jones thoughtfully, "that it really all started when Miss Barker bought a postcard of the *Mona Lisa*!"

"Oh!" said the man from the BBC weakly.